THE WINGS OF FRIENDSHIP

In the days between the great wars Jamie, the son of Lord Inchmarnock and Alejandro Medina, a Mexican orphan with a secret past and an amazing musical talent meet at school in Edinburgh. Jamie introduces Alejandro to Catriona Cameron Menmuir who notices the youngster's unusual grey blue eyes, so like those of her first husband who died in Mexico. Great changes face them all when war comes and Jamie's mother, Flora, persuades her husband to open his family home as a hospital. Jamie and Alejandro join the airforce and when they are shot down over France everyone pulls together to help one another.

THE WINGS OF FRIENDSHIP

THE WINGS OF FRIENDSHIP

by

Eileen Ramsay

Magna Large Print Books
Long Preston, North Yorkshire,
BD23 4ND, England.

British Library Cataloguing in Publication Data.

Ramsay, Eileen
   The wings of friendship.

   A catalogue record of this book is
   available from the British Library

   ISBN   0-7505-1760-3

Copyright © Eileen Ramsay 2000

Cover illustration © John Hancock by arrangement with
P.W.A. International Ltd.

The moral right of the author has been asserted

Published in Large Print 2002 by arrangement with
Mrs Eileen Ramsay

Magna Large Print is an imprint of Library Magna Books Ltd.

Printed and bound in Great Britain by
T.J. (International) Ltd., Cornwall, PL28 8RW

Episode 1

On March 29th, 1928, a Bill that gave the vote to all women over the age of twenty one went through the Houses of Parliament. Victoria Cameron Welborn let the momentous decision go by without comment: that would come later...

At present she was too distressed by the death of her old friend, and employee, Tam Menmuir to think about equal Franchise.

Why did it have to rain at the burial? Raindrops mingled with the tears on the faces of the many mourners and, their heads bowed in prayer, the men of the Angus farms ignored them both.

'Tam would have liked fine tae miss this soaking, Mr Boatman,' whispered old Robert Grey, a retired orraman or farm labourer, to the local solicitor.

'Indeed he would, Rab,' Arbuthnott Boatman replied with a smile. 'I feel he's looking down at us saying, "Get on with it, ye daft gowks and awae ben tae the fire."'

They smiled at one another, two old men

separated by education and class but joined together by their respect and love for the old man now being laid to rest.

Tam's eldest son, Davie, whose war injuries made him look frailer even than old Rab, threw a handful of rich, Angus soil on the coffin. His eyes were bright but not with tears. He had done his weeping and the tears had been for himself, not for his father.

'Goodbye, Faither,' he said softly. 'You were a guid man a' your days. I pray my son'll be able tae say the same thing aboot me when my time comes.' He turned away to leave the grave diggers to their sombre task.

One mourner, however, stayed behind. Alistair Smart had met Tam Menmuir only within the last ten years, at the wedding of Alistair's secretary, Victoria Cameron, who now owned the farm on which the old man had laboured all his days.

'You never said a word to me, Tam, but you knew how I felt about Victoria, didn't you? I could see the comfort and sympathy in your eyes. My feelings for her haven't changed, I'm afraid, though I pray every day that they will. Now I'll go to Victoria's house to help console your wife and son – but, oh Tam, who's left to console me?'

He straightened his shoulders and put on his hat. 'You were a fine man, Tam Menmuir. I'll miss your friendship.'

He looked one last time at the grave and then turned to where his motor car and his chauffeur waited.

Victoria stood at the sitting-room window and looked out at the rain-washed garden. In a way she wished that, before he had died, Tam had not found the time to prune meticulously the roses that stood stark and bare in their neat, weed free beds.

It would have been more fitting if her favourite flowers had echoed the turbulence in her own unhappy heart.

Tam had always been there, day in day out, in all the seasons. Tam, with his tobacco-less pipe clamped tightly in his teeth, his battered old hat stuck on the back of his greying head.

He was gone but she could still hear his voice talking softly to her grampa's long departed Clydesdales – 'Away ye go, hen. Hup, hup, there's ma guid lass.'

The Menmuirs and the Camerons were as entwined as rambling roses in a summer garden. Tam and her grandfather had been more than employer and worker; they had been friends for over forty years. Tam's son, Davie, had married Victoria's widowed mother.

'As far as I can see, you're the only unhappy person here, Victoria.' Her husband, Edward, had come up behind her and slipped his arms around her waist. 'There's no need to be sad, love. Tam lived a full rich life and his funeral – it was the happiest funeral I've ever attended. Does that sound silly? It's just that there was so much warmth there, so many fond and funny memories being shared. Everyone seemed to be feel privileged to have known him. Not an unkind word was spoken. Even the way he left us was gentle and peaceful. Mrs Menmuir says she's grateful he went like that, after a day with his roses.'

Victoria refused to be consoled. 'Maybe he'd still be alive if he hadn't worked so hard in his retirement.'

'Och, Victoria,' he said and she smiled as he had known she would at his use of the Scottish sound, 'he was an Angus farmer. They don't know what the word retire means. Look at Davie. If ever there was a man who should be sitting at the fire with his feet up or taking lessons on that daft piano he bought at the Stonehaven roup it's him, but...' He stopped and they looked across the room to where Davie Menmuir sat patiently tying the shoes of their younger daughter, Nancy.

Nancy waited until 'Grampa' had finished making perfect bows, scrambled from his knees and, with a smile of sheer defiance, pulled the offending shoes from her feet.

'Find, Grampa,' she ordered and her faithful servant went meekly to retrieve the shoes that she had hurled across the room.

Victoria turned back to the window and looked out at her walnut tree. It had grown well and already tight little buds were forming all along the branches.

Seven years ago she had stood in that same place hoping for signs that the tree had put down roots to anchor it safely in the fertile Angus soil. If she could just see a swelling bud, she had said to herself over and over – just one little bud to show that the tree was alive – it would be an omen. She would know then that this strange feeling inside her, a feeling that she had shared with no one, was what she hoped it was.

At the start of every day she had gone to the tree and then, one morning, as if by magic, small, tight buds swelled on every twig. A visit to the doctor, or even a chat with her mother would have answered Victoria's unspoken question far more quickly.

Somehow though, connecting the new life within her with the new life surging through the tree had bound her to the earth, to her grandfather, and to all the Camerons who had gone before. She had looked at the tree contentedly and had gone in to hurry Eddie on his way to the sheep folds.

'We're going to have a baby,' she had announced matter of factly as she dropped a kiss on top of his head.

He had shaken salt on his porridge as calmly as if she had said, 'Remember to take your coat.' Then the lovely words had slowly filtered through Eddie's foggy, early morning thoughts...

When realisation had dawned he had jumped up, spilling his porridge and crashing his chair back against the wall. And then he, who had been a sheep farmer all his life – apart from a few years as a soldier – and who was, therefore, familiar with the miracle of birth, had picked up his wife as if she was a doll and carried her to her chair in the inglenook.

'Victoria?' was all he said as he looked into her eyes and tentatively put his hard callused farmer's hand on her flat stomach.

'It'll be a wee while yet, Edward Welborn,' she said, bending over and kissing him on the nose. 'These motherless lambs will be out from under my feet long before there's another kind of baby in this house.'

She picked up one of the lambs that Eddie had restrained in a make-shift pen by the range and began to bottle feed it. The lamb sucked frenetically and its undocked tail wiggled ecstatically.

The sight was almost more than Edward could bear. After their marriage he had chosen to join Victoria, who owned Priory Farm since her father's death in Mexico, rather than look for a tenancy in his own English Lake District country.

He had worked day and night to improve the business which had been managed by a law firm since old Jock Cameron had died, introducing the Blackface sheep to previously unprofitable hill land.

The flock had thrived, and he had known it would, and the young 'foreigner' had begun to feel one with the land and the people who worked it.

And now, joy of joys, even earlier than he had hoped or expected, he was to become a father – the father of the next owner of Priory Farm.

'We'll name him Cameron, Victoria,' he said fondly. 'Or we'll put it in his name. Mr Boatmart'll know how to do it. Maybe we could put a hyphen in like the Toffs.'

'*I'm* the one who's supposed to have strange notions, Eddie. We'll do no such thing. Besides the next owner of Priory Farm could well be a girl,' – she patted her stomach affectionately – 'and she'll only change your lovely name all over again when she gets married.'

Eddie smiled complacently. 'I'm the youngest of three brothers, and my brothers have sons. Wait and see. There will be little boys running all over these hills soon.'

And Victoria had smiled and let him dream.

Now they had two daughters, Flora, named for the lady doctor who had been her mother's first lodger, and wee Nancy.

Every spring Victoria looked at her walnut tree and hoped that she too would prove as fertile and that, one day, there would be a boy to inherit the land.

'Away and rescue poor Davie before that wee madam has him exhausted,' she commanded her husband.

Chuckling, Eddie went off to fetch his daughter.

Episode 2

'Let's have a picnic, Victoria. That will cheer you up.'

Victoria smiled across at her old school friend, Elsie Morrison. 'I've been gloomy, I know. Even Eddie is getting a wee bit cross.' She refilled their cups from her second best tea-pot and tried to explain her feelings. 'Tam was my last link with my grandfather.'

'That's the silliest thing I ever heard, Victoria Cameron Welborn,' said Elsie with the security of an old and tried friendship. 'You are a link with old Jock. Your mother, your stepfather, the farm, everything is connected to everything and everyone else.'

'Of course you're right. So, we'll take the children on a picnic. Where will we go?'

Elsie evaded the question. 'We'll pretend that next Sunday, the 15th, is Easter. It's only a week late and we'll roll eggs and play games and we'll have a wonderful time.'

Because of their sadness, the family had allowed the solemn feast of Easter to pass with no more than a visit to the old Kirk.

No-one had felt like decorating eggs. Victoria looked shrewdly at her friend. 'Where?'

'Inchmarnock Woods,' said Elsie lightly as she stood up and brushed crumbs from her skirt.

Inchmarnock; the huge estate in Fife, the seat of so many childish dreams, the seat of so many adult nightmares; no, she could not return.

Victoria was eventually persuaded to agree but she did not look forward to the outing. Elsie had assembled sensible arguments; it was a beautiful place within easy driving distance; the Inchmarnocks were returning and would no doubt visit their former home at some point, perhaps they would even open it and they would expect Victoria's family to be among their guests.

'It's only a shell, Victoria.'

Victoria shook her head sadly, pain welling up inside her as it always did at thoughts of the Honorable Robert Fotheringham and his tragic death. 'It's full of ghosts.'

'Time to lay them to rest, dear, more than time.'

The children were naturally thrilled to be going in Mummy's car and then taking the ferry to Newport. It was an adventure. The picnic basket was full of all their favourites, Granny Menmuir's jam, Other-Granny's scones, and Mummy's sandwiches. And the woods? Oh, the beauty of trees tentatively unfurling baby leaves. There were trees on Priory Farm, of course, but not great avenues like these where a little girl could run and hide and perhaps, oh joy of joys, find a clump of violets or a bouquet of prim-roses.

Victoria took the offering from her daughter, Flora, and unbidden, the picture of a beautiful young boy came into her mind. He was laughing at her as she scolded him for picking the flowers. She had not known that he was the heir to all this beauty. 'They'll forgive a hero going off to war,' he had said. The frail skeletons of those flowers were still in her cherished copy of *Mansfield Park*.

She had never loved Robert, not in the way that she loved Eddie, but he was the one who had wakened her to love. He was the hero, the unattainable, the crusader.

Flora was staring at her. 'Your face is all funny.'

Victoria smiled up at the little girl. 'I was just remembering that these are my favourite flowers.'

'Good,' said Flora. 'Now Nancy and me

want our Easter eggs. We've found a hill.'

'Nancy and I,' said Victoria automatically and then she turned to Elsie. 'Should I leave their English grammar to the formidable Miss Morrison?'

'No, the parent is always the first teacher, and anyway, I might not be at the Harris by the time Flora gets there.'

'Oh, Elsie, you're not thinking of moving?'

'Not to another school, my dear, but to another career. When will the Inchmarnocks be back?' she asked abruptly as they turned a corner on the path and saw the great house before them.

'Goodness knows. They had to arrange factors and managers for their station. A farm's not a farm down under, it's a station. I keep seeing trains instead of sheep.' Victoria smiled to herself as she saw visions of great straining locomotives being herded by sheep dogs.

'Lady Inchmarnock will probably be very useful to me,' Elsie said. 'I hope they don't take too long. Sometimes the idle rich are just too damned idle.'

'They can't make the ship go any faster, Elsie,' pointed out Victoria. 'But tell me, what can Doctor Flora do for you?'

'Eggs,' demanded Nancy, holding out a

very grubby hand.

They had to wait until the two little girls had had their fun and were at last seated under a great beach tree and eating broken eggs, and no doubt some egg shells.

Victoria had opened the old picnic basket with its white cups and saucers and its little tea plates. She poured hot strong tea from the thermos flask and they sat back, sipped the refreshing brew and smiled at one another.

Victoria looked at her daughters and her heart filled with love for them. She raised her eyes to look up into the branches of the magnificent trees. No ghostly figures lingered among the new leaves. No voices murmured of love or pain or regret. The only sound was the quiet talk and the laughter of the children.

'You were right, Elsie. Time we came back.' She offered Elsie the packet of carefully wrapped sandwiches. 'Now, what's this about career changes?'

'I've decided to run for Parliament.'

Elsie had always been interested in local government. She had been an active suffragette and Victoria had assumed that her friend's ambitions had all been fulfilled when women were granted the vote. But this...?

'Parliament? In London?' Victoria gasped.

'Well, there isn't one in Edinburgh, more's the pity, but one thing at a time, and your Doctor Currie, or Lady Inchmarnock, is the very person to help me.'

'But Doctor Flora left the country to avoid scandal. She's hardly likely to want to walk right back into controversy.'

Elsie made an inelegant sound that could have been described as a snort. 'Piffle, Victoria. Flora Currie became a doctor when her class thought that a frightful thing to do – naked human bodies, my God – and then she married a divorced man. She's just the one to help me. We'll make a great team. Now, high time these two were tidied up and home to bed. Eddie will be sighing over your absence.'

Immediately Victoria smiled. 'Yes, he will, won't he,' she agreed complacently.

The foreman chose to allow the wall to be demolished just as Catriona and Davie were explaining the proceedings to Bessie Menmuir, Davie's mother.

Catriona waited until the rumbles had stopped and the thick cloud of dust had almost settled – on her hair, her new coat with its lovely fur collar, and on Davie.

She pulled her husband away from where the wall had been and walked him to the pavement since the wind was moving the dust in the other direction. 'Are you all right, Davie?' she asked anxiously.

Davie coughed a little, took out a spotless white handkerchief and blew his nose. 'Fit as a fiddle,' he said. 'What did you think of that, Mam?'

Bessie looked at the pile of rubbish. 'I'm sure you know what you're doing, Catriona lass. You're the most capable woman I've ever known and if you say a grand new garage is going to appear on this heap of old boulders, I suppose I'll believe you.'

'1928 is a grand time to be alive, Mrs Menmuir. See that big machine over there? It'll sweep this lot up in no time and there will be a nice flat area for rebuilding. The good walls we'll keep...'

She broke off as a car drew up and her old friend and lawyer, Arbuthnott Boatman, emerged followed by her son, Andrew. The boy headed straight for the debris but Davie put a warning arm around his stepson's shoulders.

'No very safe, Andrew lad.'

The boy obeyed but it was obvious that he would have loved nothing more than to be

21

climbing all over the rubble.

'I tell you what,' said Mr Boatman. 'We'll go into that little café over there and watch from the window while we enjoy a cup of tea. It's not Lamb's Coffee House, Catriona, but it looks respectable enough.'

'Very helpful to the business,' he decided as a few minutes later they were seated at a table in the window watching the workman.

'How, Mr Boatman?' asked Andrew. 'How can this wee place help my Mum's garage.'

'Clients need a cup of tea while they're waiting for their cars to be mended, Andrew. A wee cup of tea and a scone help pass the time very nicely, does it not, Mistress Menmuir?'

Mrs Menmuir looked dubiously at her scone. 'Depends on the scones, Mr. Boatman.'

Catriona smiled fondly at her mother-in-law. 'You'll be safe at home baking your own delicious scones, Mother Menmuir, and our customers will be quite happy with these.' She looked as if she had been going to say more but there was another rumble from across the road as some of the corrugated tin roof fell down on the debris that had been the wall. 'Oh, Arbuthnott Boatman, have you let me go too far this time? It was you who saw the potential in the Blackness House but it was not near so bad as this and Davie and his dad and the others were able to do all the repairs.'

'Without vision the people perish,' quoted the old lawyer. 'Catriona, I'm sure Davie would have had a go at fixing up this place too but you can afford to have other people do the work now. I must admit when you first told me you wanted to run a garage I had some doubts, but this is a grand location, and this scone ... well, it would run away and hide if placed beside one of yours, Mistress Menmuir, but it's as good as my housekeeper makes, although I'll deny I said that, Andrew.' He turned back to Catriona. 'By the way, I saw an advertisement in the courier this morning for a Morris for a mere £55. There was one too for a van, an excellent purchase, Davie, if you're thinking of helping with small removals.'

Davie took his time answering but he always did so no one worried. 'I'll need tae ask Eddie tae have a look. He's the mechanical genius in the family, but forbye, two more cars sounds like we'll need tae hire another driver. Are we no spending too much too fast?'

Arbuthnott Boatman handed his cream

filled cake to young Andrew. 'You'll have Andrew here before long. He'll be your right hand man.'

'I will not,' said the boy, his mouth full of cake. 'When this garage and the boarding house are mine, I'm going to live like a Toff, like you, Mr Boatman. I'm not doing any work.'

Silenced, all four adults looked at ten year old Andrew. Arbuthnott Boatman thought, not for the first time, that although in looks he favoured his grandfather, old Jock Cameron, in behaviour he was more like his father, John.

Catriona laughed shakily. 'If you grow up like Mr Boatman, Andrew, you'll do fine.'

Davie was troubled. 'Andrew, the garage and the boarding house won't belong to you. There's Victoria, and the girls. All the family share our hard work and our good times.'

Andrew finished his cake. 'Victoria has the farm and those wee lassies are spoiled rotten anyway. They don't need any more. I'm the one nobody thinks about.'

Catriona wondered if this was the time to tell Andrew that Victoria had always promised to share the farm with him. They had the same father, although he had died before Andrew was born, but Victoria was John Cameron's legitimate heir, and Andrew was not.

'Let's go over to the demolition work, Andrew,' said Mrs Menmuir. 'Davie, you stay here and have another of those *wonderful* scones. Those lungs of yours have had enough dust for one day.'

The anticipation of watching still more destruction made young Andrew forget his grievances and he took his 'Granny' Menmuir's hand as they hurried across the street.

Mrs Menmuir had, for eight of Andrew's ten years, felt strongly that the youngster needed a good wallop but like all good grannies she had kept out of the family's affairs. How could a laddie brought up by her Davie, the world's kindest and most gentle man, and by Catriona, be as self centred as young Andrew was? There was no truth to his statement that he was the last thought on his elders' minds; he was, in her considered opinion, consulted and considered far too much. She herself had begun life in service at a big house and had learned one phrase in French from her employer; *Pas devant les enfants*. There had been far too much *in front of the children* in her son's

25

household. She closed her mouth firmly and her hand even more tightly on young Andrew's hand and hauled him quickly, despite her advanced years, across the road.

Sister Mercedes had a phonograph and she was playing a record for the older children. The voice of the young Italian tenor, Beniamino Gigli, floated out across the superbly carved furniture and whispered into the heavy velvet curtains. She saw the rapt look on young Xandro's face and smiled as the record began to wind down.

'An incredible voice, Alejandro,' she said.

'Oh, I didn't notice, Madre, but what a pianist. Who is he?'

Sister Mercedes stood up, much to the relief of most of the children who preferred old Sister Stella Maria who sang folk songs and accompanied herself on the guitar. 'The finest tenor voice the world has ever heard, boy, and "I didn't notice" says he. Go to bed at once.'

The children fled but, apart from Xandro who went all the way up the wooden staircases to the boys' dormitory, they did not go far. Sister was not angry with them. They had listened to the unintelligible screeching of the Italian with resigned if not pained expressions and they could now enjoy their chocolate and sugary churros with light consciences. Sister Mercedes appeared at the door of her study and caught the slowest boy.

'Pedro, tell Xandro I want to see him, now.'

It was Pedros's turn to flee, up, up, up. When Sister spoke in such a voice it was best to do her bidding quickly. Poor Xandro. She was going to slap his legs and all because he did not appreciate Italian opera.

Xandro, too, thought he was to be punished and entered the study in fear. The old nun understood immediately.

'Xandro, querido mio, dear child, you should know I do not punish twice for one sin. Besides you did nothing wrong to prefer the pianist to the singer. I was in the wrong to force my likes upon you.'

He grinned at her. 'I like your singer, Sister, but I like better when I understand the words. Music is ... I don't know how to explain,' he finished hanging his head.

'A universal language, Alejandro,' she said but although he smiled, she knew that he did not really understand.

She looked down at the dark little head so

like Lucia's. The boy was like Lucia, proud, stubborn, but so loving, so generous, so anxious to be loved. She sighed and then sighed again as her long fingers found the heavy parchment in her black serge pocket.

'Sit down, Xandro, no, querido, here near me.'

He sat down on the sofa beside her and smiled at the nun out of those strange grey blue eyes, the Scotsman's eyes.

'Alejandro, the time has come to tell you a little about yourself and to explain why I have been so strict, so anxious for you to study and learn.' She got up and walked to the chest in the corner and Xandro, for some reason, was aware of the rustling of her skirts, like wind through grass, he thought, or maybe through trees.

'These belong to you, child,' she said and handed him a carefully wrapped packet.

Inside was a heavy gold wedding ring encrusted with deep green emeralds and a crucifix studded with diamonds and pearls.

He held them in his little hands and looked at her, sudden fear in his eyes.

'They belonged to your mother, La Dama Lucia Alcantarilla-Medina. I have not used them to feed you. His Excellency, the Bishop, agreed with me that they might be needed to finance your education.' She sighed. 'Xandro, your mother was a member of a noble family, and I know very little but...' She thought again. How often had she gone over possible conversations with the child? The right words would not come, no matter how she prayed, or thought them out again and again. How could she say, You are the result of a misalliance. Your family is ashamed of you. I think your grandfather wanted you to disappear. He would not have given me the jewels had he wanted you ... dead. 'Xandro, your family ... you ... they... Your mother, Lucia, was so beautiful and so very young. She married a man of whom your grandfather, Don Alejandro, did not approve. Your parents are both dead, but you have an uncle, Don Alvaro, who has paid for your upkeep all these years. He wants now to remove you from my care. You are a gentleman, Xandro. You must go to school.'

'No, I go to school already, with you. I speak French as well as Spanish. I can do sums, I know about great artists and musicians and I promise to listen to Gigli. I promise.'

Sobbing, he put his little face down in her black serge lap and she smothered the impulse to lift him in her arms. God had given him to her for too long already. She was a nun, a Mother Superior. There were so many orphans all over Mexico and she had given too much to this one. 'Sit up at once, ungrateful boy. An Alcantarilla-Medina would die before he lost control of his emotions. Behave yourself.'

He sat up and rubbed his eyes with hard little knuckles and the gesture hurt her as it hurt his eyes. 'Your uncle is coming to take you to Mexico City. I have told him of your interest in the piano and he says you may continue your studies under someone more capable than I. Now join the others for supper and then say your prayers and go to bed. Don Alvaro will be here tomorrow.'

He stood up and moved slowly towards the door. She could have been strong had he not turned, had she not seen the beautifully shaped mouth quiver, those unusual eyes fill with tears he fought to conquer. She held out her arms and he ran to her and buried his head in the folds of serge while she rocked him and murmured soothing nothings just as mothers have done since the beginning of time.

At last he stopped sobbing and lay quietly listening to her heart beat.

'Mi hijo, my son,' she whispered and then banished the word for ever from her lips. He was not her son, not her child. She had been a bride, a bride of Christ, and had chosen happily, willingly, not to bear children. 'But this child, sweet saviour,' she prayed, 'he was delivered into my very hands. You gave him to me to love and cherish.'

She held the boy away from her so that she could look into those sea grey eyes. 'Xandro, you will go from me tomorrow, from my side, querido, but never from my heart. You must write and tell me of your studies and we will see one another again. Don Alvaro is a good man and his friends are fine people. You must relish your new life, accept all the challenges and when it is hard, and life is, my dear child, remember that I am here and that I love you.' And then she remembered again that she was a nun and she added, 'As do all the other sisters and the other children.'

Xandro sobbed one last time, accepted her sensible handkerchief and dried his face. He smiled at her. 'Goodbye, Madre mia. I will be a brave boy.'

Xandro, however, was a very small boy and he was too traumatised by his sudden departure from the orphanage, the only home he had ever known, and from Sister Mercedes, to enjoy the novelty of driving in a real motor car across the great plain of Mexico. He had tried again to cling to the nun's skirts and, hiding her own heartbreak, she had pulled his hands from her. He had looked up into the austere face of this man who was his uncle and had seen nothing there to reassure him.

Alvaro had looked at the child who should have grown up to be the pride of his family and had seen, not an aristocrat, but an urchin with badly cut hair and clothes that had seen better days and other owners.

'Have I made yet another mistake?' Don Alvaro asked himself as he drove quickly towards Mexico City.

His chauffeur had wondered that his employer should go on a journey without being properly attended but Alvaro was aware that his chauffeur like every other servant of the Alcantarilla-Medina family reported directly to the head of the family, his older brother, Don Jose-Luis.

'And he must never know where the boy is.'

They drove into Mexico City and, despite his worries, Xandro gazed excitedly out of the window. Goodness, what a place was this, buildings everywhere, cars, lights, horse drawn carriages, and people, and oh, the noise, never had he heard such noise. They stopped at one of the city's lesser hotels, a hostelry which did not enjoy the patronage of the Alcantarillas. Don Alvaro ordered a meal and was pleased to note that the child's manners were perfect. Alvaro ordered icecream – his nieces loved it – and laughed out loud at the expression of surprise and then pleasure on the little boy's face.

Xandro smiled too when he saw the relaxed look on the rather stern face and Alvaro's heart contracted as he saw his little sister's smile. 'The eyes are wrong; they are *his* eyes but we will not blame the child.'

They did not stay in the hotel but drove on into the night. The boy fell asleep and Alvaro covered him with a fur rug: nights can be cold in Mexico.

At last they arrived on the outskirts of Puebla and Alvaro drove confidently through the narrow, winding streets until he came to large gate set in a wall. Bougain-villaea rioted over the wall and Alvaro avoided its thorns as he looked for the bell pull.

An old man appeared at a run and threw open the gate bowing his head vigorously at the same time.

There were lights on in the house and Alvaro could see the flicker of candlelight from the dining room as he drove to the front door. It opened before he reached it and he saw his old friend waving his arms in a semaphore of greeting.

'Alvaro, old friend, how good to see you. Where is the child?'

The child had wakened as the car door was opened and the light fell on his face.

'Come along, Alejandro. This is Senor Himenez who is going to look after you.'

Xandro stumbled from the car and rubbed his eyes to try to chase away the sleep.

A friendly face was smiling down at him. 'Come along, young man. My wife has run upstairs to draw you a nice hot bath.'

Obediently Xandro followed the two men up the wide stairs and into the cool tiled hall. They walked into a dimly lit room where candles burned on a piano. The child stopped, looked at it in surprise and then moved towards it.

'We are not collecting finger prints today, young Xandro,' laughed Senor Himenez but

Xandro did not hear. Never had he seen such an instrument. He looked around the room in rising joy. There was an organ against a wall, just like the one in the Convent Chapel and there were guitar-like instruments piled up near a sofa.

'Those are tiples, Xandro, a very old instrument and, I think, with a purer sound than the guitar.'

But Xandro had been drawn back to the grand piano and he put out his hand and caressed a note.

Alvaro moved angrily as if to stop him but Senor Himenez stopped him and together they watched the boy. One note, then another, and then as his fear left him he played a little melody with his right hand. Senor Himenez went forward quietly and pulled out the stool and the child perched on it, his thin little legs swinging, and added the left hand accompaniment.

'Someone has taught him well, Alvaro.'

'Mercedes.'

'Good gracious, good gracious, good gracious. The child has been driving in this heat all day and instead of bath and bed, you make him play the piano.'

The men and the boy looked up at the voice and saw Senora Himenez swooping down on Xandro. She took his hand and docilely he followed her to the stair. There he stopped and turned to face the two men.

'I can play the piano?' he asked.

'Yes, Xandro, I am a music teacher.'

'Good,' said the boy quietly. 'I will stay.'

Tilbury dock on a wet morning is not the most encouraging 'Welcome to Britain.' Flora Currie Fotheringham, Lady Inchmarnock, shook the raindrops from her very fetching hat and looked around for her young son.

'Why is it, Sandy,' she asked her husband who was standing breathing in great gulps of the brine scented air, 'that it's raining every time I arrive in England? The season doesn't matter and it doesn't matter where I have been, I arrive in England and ruin my best hat.'

'I like it, Mummy,' said the Honorable James Fotheringham who at great peril to life and limb was hanging over the side of the ship trying to catch as much rain as possible on his tongue. 'Not your hat, though I'm sure that's very pretty,' he added hastily, 'but the rain. I bet children in England never need to take baths. Is that right, Daddy?'

'Absolutely, old man.'

'Sandy.' Lady Inchmarnock was not pleased at the levity shown by her husband but she saw the smile of sheer glee that passed between her menfolk and realised that, not for the first time, they were teasing her.

She turned again to look for their chauffeur and tried to stifle a sigh. Jamie would have to go to school and Sandy, who had enjoyed sharing every day of this precious child's life, would miss him unbearably. She would too, of course, but she was prepared. Perhaps it was her medical training?

'We old soldiers soldier on, old girl.'

So he had known what she was thinking: he always did. How could she think for a moment that he could not cope. He had lost his beloved Robert to the horror of the war and he had coped. She smiled. She had been there, most of the time, to help him survive that loss. She was here now. She would always be here.

'Come down before you fall down, Jamie.'

He made a half hearted effort to obey. 'Oh, look Mummy, there's my trunk. Good Heavens, Daddy, is all that luggage ours? What did you bring, Mummy?'

'Everything that mattered to me in Australia, Jamie,' said Lady Inchmarnock as she led him down the gangplank.

Lord Inchmarnock's London solicitor had had the foresight to send two large cars to the docks. They were not big enough.

'You go on to the hotel with Jamie and the first lot, darling. Get all your phone calls done.'

That would give him time to come to grips with the reality. He had vowed never again to live in Britain. He had sold most of his property that was not entailed and his cousin, who had expected to become Lord Inchmarnock, was living in his London house. He knew the boy was there to cut him out, of course, and he had accepted the fact, but here they were again because Flora thought the child was becoming a little savage. Women, just because the boy had never seen an opera.

'Poor old Jamie,' thought his father as he watched the little hand waving until the motor was out of sight. 'Now running wild will be reserved for school holidays and I'll make sure they're as wild as you like. But Flora's right. Two hours a day over the wireless and as much tuition as she could get him to sit still for ... not enough. We

38

could stay in London, turf Thomas out of the house and find a decent day school.'

He stopped short as he remembered that he had never really liked London. He and Robert had loved Scotland and, although they were perfectly civil and probably better friends than when they had been married, Julia lived in London. Flora would meet his first wife everywhere, at dinners, lunches, fashion shows. He laughed, 'but rarely at the opera.' Julia went to the opera only to be seen. Flora went to lose herself in the sound.

'No school near Inchmarnock but I can't live there again, ever. Edinburgh. We'll go to Edinburgh. There'll be a decent day school there for our little boy: we can keep him with us a while yet.'

Flora smiled when he told her of his decision. She had already instructed a solicitor in Edinburgh to find them a house and to obtain brochures from several of the schools. She had not thought of opera. She had thought of Dundee and the Menmuirs and her friends and former patients. Edinburgh is no distance at all from Dundee, not in these days of fast cars.

Flora had been one of the first lady doctors in Dundee to have a car. She made a list.

1. House
2. School – (day).
3. Car

Those were the priorities. She looked out of the window and sighed as still more rain hurled itself against the glass.

'Never satisfied, Flora,' she scolded herself. 'In Australia you longed for rain. And I am satisfied. This new life is not going to be easy for any of us but I have Sandy and my precious Jamie. What did Sandy say? "Old soldiers soldier on." We will. We'll soldier on.'

Dr Flora Currie, Lady Inchmarnock, looked forward to the fray.

Episode 3

1933 Edinburgh

Rain, rain, and more rain. The novelty of rain had soon worn off but like most children the Honorable James Fotheringham quickly accepted whatever was dished out to him and that included weather. Rain was a nuisance in that it interrupted tennis and swimming outings and it made hockey and rugby uncomfortable. Jamie hated lying awake at night listening to rain beating against the windows and knowing that all too soon he was going to have to leave his warm if rather spartan bed, wash in luke-warm water – the hot always seemed to be gone by the time it was his turn for the spray bath – and then run up the path under the trees which delighted in sending freezing drops of water down his neck, to sit gently steaming in the dining room while he demolished his breakfast. Once fed and dry the return journey had to be made.

Oh yes, the Honourable James Fothering-ham hated school. The little day school where they had placed him upon their return from Australia was not too awful – but this place. He looked around the dorm, swarming, as he told his parents, with low life – (all similarly placed little boys) and groaned.

Every third Saturday afternoon his mother filled him with Pheemie's best cooking and assured him that he was the most cherished boy in the entire world and then drove him back through the gates of this ... prison.

How could she say 'I love you' with one breath and 'It's time to go' with another?

41

Pondering on the inconsistencies of adults the Honorable James fell asleep.

Next afternoon, Jamie, together with lots of other little boys shivering in brown and magenta games attire, trotted in the rain from their houses to the playing fields. Jamie stopped as the main school towered up before him and swore softly under his breath. It really was the most ghastly building, not really a school, not really a castle, a Victorian nightmare of towers and curlicues. He stuck out his tongue at the gargoyles glaring down at him warning him that he had better get a move on. That funny foreign kid had stopped beside him to tie his boots. What must he think of it? Better not to ask. He was too good at answering any questions with his fists – awful little blighter.

They ran on and reached the fields and old Brewster, sadist that he was, made them strip to shorts and start running round the perimeter. One way of keeping warm. The rain was heavier and colder. It was what his father called sleet. Jamie tried to run faster but he certainly was no match for the little foreigner.

They formed into teams and the games master tried to instil the virtues of team work into cold little boys who only wanted to get the whole miserable episode over. They dreamed of cocoa and toast in houses.

'That way, Medina. Don't you understand anything, boy.'

Brewster was furious, running up and down the field like one demented. Well, he was demented. They all were or they would not be Public School teachers.

The foreigner had the ball and was running.

'Yippee,' yelled Jamie. 'Go for it.'

It was a captain's dream come true. The fastest man in the Lower School was on his team and he was running into touch.

And then the sleet turned to snow.

The boy with the ball stopped abruptly to look at wonder, at magic. Never before had he seen this phenomenon that he had read about in books. It was beautiful. He wanted to taste it.

What he tasted was the mud of the field as a whole host of dirty, cold little boys, blinded by snow, ran into him and into each other and fell in a squealing mass into the churned up mess. And then fists as well as snow began to fly as they began to pummel one another and especially that stupid blighter who should have been a hero and was now a definite nuisance that no team captain would ever pick, EVER.

And Jamie Fotheringham, captain of his side for the first time, did something that he was to regret. He hit a man when he was down. He punched the muddy little face that peered up at him and shouted, 'Why didn't you stay in your own country, you absolute moron.'

The boy wiped the blood from his nose with the back of his hand and then threw himself at Jamie and it took three boys on each side to pull them apart.

'Savages,' muttered the games master as he marched them up to the school where, once they were clean, he meted out severe but just punishment. 'You, at least, Fotheringham, are supposed to be a gentleman.'

It was not an auspicious start to any friendship. Jamie, however, had been brought up by loving parents and his conscience troubled him. Medina had been on his knees when he had punched him.

'Not cricket,' decided Jamie. 'The parents wouldn't like it.'

He was too embarrassed to say anything though and the days went by and the funny foreign kid made little effort to mix. He kept himself to himself and Jamie shrugged and ignored him but he did not like the look almost of contempt that young Medina gave him.

'So, he doesn't like me and I don't like him.'

Then one day he found Medina alone on the famous Green Walk. He looked miserable and although he was warmly dressed, he was shivering. Why on earth was he outside freezing when he could be with the others in the Common Room?

'Because we're mean to him.' He answered his own question.

He stopped in front of the boy. 'You must feel the cold,' he began. 'I did at first when we came back from Australia.'

'I have the warm clothes but they are so scratchy.'

Jamie scratched his tweed covered thigh. 'You're right. Very scratchy. I hardly wore anything in Australia and never tweed.'

They jumped to their feet as they saw their housemaster approaching. 'Well done, Fotheringham,' he said, 'After your initial lapse I hope you'll have a civilising affect on young Medina here.'

The boys watched him sail proudly down the path before they sat down. 'He's angry because I am fighting always but I am civilised already.'

'My mother thinks I need civilising. That's why she sent me here. I just know my father would have let me stay in Australia on our ranch. What do your people do?'

'My people?'

'Parents.'

'I have no parents but I have ... had an uncle who had a ranch in Mexico. He was going to take me to see it one day ... and then his car crashed in the rains and they sent me here instead. It was in his Will.'

Jamie's loving heart swelled. No parents and an uncle who died. He thought of his own doting parents. 'You know what, Medina. Let's bury the hatchet and be friends and we'll civilise each other.'

He held out his thin little white hand and the other boy looked at it and at Jamie's face and then put out his strong brown one. He smiled. What *bury the hatchet* meant he had absolutely no idea.

'Friends,' he said, 'and we will mix our blood so that it is for ever.'

Jamie gulped when he saw the sharp little penknife. They'd get killed if anyone saw them with a knife. Bravely he held out his hand and Medina sliced into his finger and then, without a qualm, into one of his own. Solemnly the little boys pressed the bleed-

46

ing fingers together and they did not see disaster bearing down upon them as the house master strode back to the main college.

'I don't know, Headmaster,' Mr Patterson reported later. 'I hope a sore posterior will remind that child to behave like a gentleman, but the little blighter didn't even whimper.'

'Indian blood, probably, but he's a fine musician, so Mr Havergal says. We'll make a gentleman of him yet.'

The housemaster had not a musical bone in his body and therefore had little respect for Henry Havergal, one of the finest musicians ever to teach in a Public School. 'You don't believe all that nonsense about music having a civilising effect, Headmaster.'

Dr Ashcroft sighed. So difficult to deal with a man with no sense of humour. He turned from the window where he had been watching boys of assorted sizes chatting and playing on the great steps that lead to the road and thence to the outside world. He loved to look at the beauty and history that was Edinburgh stretched out before him and a view of his city together with some of the boys to whom he was totally dedicated was a particular joy.

'Put a log on the fire, there's a good chap,' he said while he sat down at the heavy oak desk he had inherited from his predecessor. The desk was turned from the window. Otherwise the headmaster felt sure he would be tempted to spend too much time losing himself in the view of the city.

'Young Medina is from one of the finest Mexican families, as far as I know. There's a bit of a mystery but I believe Alcantarilla-Medina is not the whole of his surname.'

'Long enough as it is, surely?'

'Indeed, but I believe Latins add on the names of wives to the surname – very complicated, and then again I have an instinct that tells me he is not Mexican at all. Well, perhaps not so far as that but, look at his eyes, Paterson. No pure bred Spaniard ever had eyes that colour, and why Fettes, I ask myself. There must be decent schools in Mexico or the United States for that matter. Why uproot a little boy from everything he has ever known and send him to a cold country thousands of miles away if there is no good reason.'

'Perhaps it's the fame of our music department.'

Dr Ashcroft bowed acknowledgement. Yes,

the fame of the music department – and many other departments – could easily have spread to the Colonies but...

'His guardian is Director of the Conservatory in Mexico City.'

Mr Patterson who knew less than Jamie Fotheringham about Mexico smiled complacently. 'Mexico City. A backwater in the third world, Headmaster. But at least this director knew enough to send him here. I saw that young Fotheringham has taken him up. That should help too. Alex has no family for exeats, does he? All to the good if Lord Inchmarnock were to invite the boy to visit. Mind you, I would have to confess to his lordship that so far Medina has been a poor influence on Jamie.'

'They're little boys, Housemaster. Little boys grow up.'

Mr Patterson was determined to get the last word. 'But not always into gentlemen, Headmaster.'

Catriona Menmuir was determined to win this battle. Her son, Andrew, was just as determined that he would be the victor.

'I'm fifteen. All my friends have left the school and I'm going to leave too. I can be a great help in the garage, Mum.'

Catriona had worked too hard to have her son throw away the chance of a good education. She looked at him now and thought of his sister at the same age, so anxious to learn and unable to go on because of lack of money. Now she had worked and worked to make sure that Andrew should want for nothing, especially a university education, and he was throwing her sacrifices and Victoria's back in their faces. She wished him small again so that she could smack him.

'It's very kind of you to worry about us, Andrew,' she said carefully, 'but your father and I want the best for you, and that means staying on and getting your higher leaving certificates and then going to the university.'

'He's not my father,' said Andrew spitefully and thus sealed his fate. For the first time in his life Catriona slapped him hard. No matter what he had done – and there had been some episodes that he did not want to recall at length – he had been able to deflect her anger. He stared at her in shock.

'He is the best father you could ever have had, Andrew Menmuir; since before you were even born he cared for you, and for me and Victoria, and if you grow up anything like him, you'll be a fine man. Now listen to me and understand what I am saying. God has given you a brain and all I ask is that you use it. There is no job for you in the garage or the boarding house, not now, not ever. We want you to better yourself. Get your highers and then we'll talk again. I won't force you into doing something you hate and maybe in a few years if you say you want to be a mechanic, then we'll see that you're properly trained.'

Andrew looked at her and wondered if he should start to cry. She could never refuse him anything when he cried. That knowledge of his mother's weakness had served him in good stead.

'Oh, Mummy, I never meant to do it,' he had wept when discovered in some meanness or act of cruelty.

Should he try it now? Then he saw the set of her jaw.

'I'm sorry I said that ... about Dad. Don't tell him and I'll never say it again.'

'Don't even think it.'

'Mum.' He threw his arms around her ample waist. 'Mum, I want to help you and Dad in the garage. It's going to be mine and I should learn everything so I can help on Dad's bad days. Please.'

Catriona weakened. How well he knew how to get round her. She would be firm. She had to be firm. She pushed his hands away. 'You'll help us best by doing well at school. Jimmy Sinclair out at the Priory has it in his head to be a doctor and even wee Flora talks about being a teacher and her only thirteen.'

What can I say to her, thought Andrew. What did Nellie Sinclair's brats mean to him? They were the children of his sister's cleaner. Never mind that he had played with them and his two nieces for years. But he knew who he was now and he was taking second place to no-one. The garage would be his and maybe the boarding house – although he never told his friends that his mother took in boarders. Miss Davis, Classics teacher at the Harris, could hardly be called a boarder. When he grew up he would buy a big car and smoke cigars and he would never work the way Davie did. In his mind he had stopped thinking of Davie as his father and he wished Victoria had never told him about his real father. It was when wee Nancy was christened. Somehow Victoria had known that sometimes he would like to be small again, the centre of attention.

'Girls aren't much use,' he had said. 'There are far too many girls on this farm already. They can't be farmers.'

'Nowadays girls can be almost anything they want to be, Andrew. I would have made a good farmer if Grampa had left it to me as he intended.'

And then Andrew had asked all about the farm and Victoria had told him, haltingly, as much as she thought he was old enough to understand.

Andrew had been quietly furious. Not only had he no real right to a share in Priory Farm, he had no real father. He and Victoria had the same father but Victoria was born when they were married and he was born after they were divorced: years after, Victoria had admitted in embarrassment. Poor Andrew was too stunned and frightened by the little his sister thought it right to tell him that he decided not to ask his mother for an explanation; he did not want to know any more. For her part, Catriona was glad that he seemed to be satisfied with Victoria's explanations and, thankfully, decided not to worry about it.

Now that Andrew was fifteen and aware of the meaning of the word illegitimate, he worried and fretted even more, but he sought no comfort from his family. His comfort came in knowing that, if his mother had no right to Priory Farm, she certainly owned both the boarding house and the garage and, he was absolutely determined, both would one day belong to him.

'I'll be richer than anyone one day,' decided young Andrew, 'and then they'll be sorry.'

Why his family were to be made sorry, he did not really understand.

In the meantime he would stay at the Harris and he would pass all his exams and his mother would be prouder of him than she was of Victoria.

But oh for it to be 1939 when he would be twenty one and free to do anything and go anywhere. He would show everyone then.

More than anyone else, Elsie Morrison understood Andrew. She understood him because he was like her, full of ambition. When she resigned her teaching post at the Harris Academy, she even felt slightly guilty about leaving Andrew without her guidance. But, she decided, she had to think of the greater good. And the greater good was that Dundee should have a second woman Member of Parliament.

Elsie looked out onto rain lashed streets and watched the frenzied bowing of the leafless trees. Oh, to have the power of that wind, to make everything bow before her – for their own good. There were thousands of people unemployed in Dundee, many of them women. The poverty all around was horrifying. Even out there on the street on a day like this were children without shoes, women without coats. Probably they were going home to crowded tenements where there was little or no heating, and unless they were lucky, little or no food.

Unaware of any irony, Elsie threw another log on the blazing fire, and then walked along her carpeted corridor to the kitchen where her daily help, Morag, had left her tray of tea.

Elsie Morrison was determined to be Dundee's first woman Labour Member of Parliament. Florence Horsburgh, who had replaced the prohibitionist, Edwin Scrymgeour, was – no one would deny it – a great lady and had worked long and hard for the working class. In fact, the mill and factory women had voted en bloc to send Florence Horsbrugh to Westminster. Dundee's first woman MP was, however, also Dundee's first Conservative MP, and Elsie had decided she would be its last. Dundee needed the Labour candidate, Elsie Morrison. Nothing must get in the way of fulfilling that ambition, and nothing included Kenneth Scott.

Elsie sighed and carried her tray into the living room. She would fortify herself and then she would be able to write to Ken. It was the coward's way but if she heard his voice, she knew she would give in.

Before she had finished her tasty meal the telephone on the table in the hall interrupted her.

'Elsie, can we count on some of your farmer friends supporting us at the meeting tonight. We need to broaden our horizon, think bigger.' The abrasive voice was that of her boss on the local council, Dave Roberts.

Elsie sighed again. While she was thinking of Ken she did not want to speak to Dave or to acknowledge how his strutting masculinity affected her, disturbed her.

'The Welborns will come, Dave, but they're really coming just for the chance of an evening out. Dundee's problems aren't theirs.'

'The Farmers Union is a strong body and Welborn is a delegate. Let him hear you speak on a political issue. All he knows is that you're good at cooing sweet nothings to those wee lassies of his. Very important to let yourself be heard as a strong woman.'

Ken wanted her to be helpless and feminine, didn't he? Wasn't that why he wanted her to give up politics and marry him? Dave was happy to acknowledge her political talents but he didn't want to marry her, did he? He had never spoken of marriage, or love.

'Eddie knows I was Deputy Head of Department at the Harris, Dave. You don't get positions like that by fluttering your eyelashes.'

'Oh, don't you?' he laughed and put the phone down before she could answer him. That was another of the annoying things about Dave. He never let her have the last word.

Elsie went back to her interrupted toasting. There was something so soothing about sitting in front of a fire toasting crumpets. Memories of childhood days flooded back: she saw herself and her mother trudging back from Suffragette meetings, buoyed up by the words of women like Dundee's own Lila Clunas, who had actually spent three whole weeks in Holloway jail. Then into the house where her father and brothers would greet them with laughing, loving scorn.

'Any of you new women capable of toasting muffins?' they would tease and every time she responded, snatching the toasting fork and assuring them that women could do anything and stay feminine while they did it.

None of them to see her now; all dead, most of her brothers in the war to end all wars. That was what she would fight for when she entered Parliament. She would force the Government to ignore the antics of that man, Hitler, who had come from nowhere to become Chancellor of Germany and who had abolished Freedom of Speech and was seemingly doing other unimaginable things. He was Germany's problem and no Scottish boys should die to depose him. If the Germans allowed him to stay in office, then they deserved him.

'After all,' Elsie assured herself as she went to her desk to write to Kenneth, 'we wouldn't tolerate a man like Hitler. Neither will the Germans. The tales that come out of Germany are all grossly exaggerated.'

She had to believe that. She had to believe. Otherwise all those deaths were for nothing. The unhappy thoughts strengthened her resolve. She would not think of Ken's gentleness, of the way his eyes smiled at her, of the lovely feeling in the pit of her stomach when she heard his voice. Elsie unscrewed the lid from the bottle of ink and filled her new fountain pen.

Dear Ken,
It's no use. I have thought and thought and I have come to the conclusion that I could not make you happy. I want to be of some use in the world, Ken. I NEED to be of use. If I go against all my principles and give up my political career to marry you, then I would be wronging everyone, especially you and me.

There are children in your classroom who will go home to a cold empty house. There will be no loving smells of nourishing food meeting them as they climb their tenement stairs. These children cry out to me, my dearest, and I cannot ignore them. If I lift my head from this paper I can see the pavement outside. Isn't this what is termed a NICE area, Ken, and yet children are running home, without coats, without shoes. Will a loving mother greet them or will they meet with blows because poverty breeds anger and intolerance and often it is the children who suffer for the misery of their fathers. A fair wage for a day's work and jobs for all who want them. That will be my battle cry.

It will be better if you do not come to see me, and do not use the telephone to contact me. My mind is quite made up.
Your friend,
Elsie Morrison.

She sealed the letter and put on her coat and hat.

If it were done when 'tis done, then 'twere well it were done quickly.

She would brave the weather to post the letter for if she waited until the rain stopped her resolution might founder and the letter might never be sent. But she must not keep hoping against all hope that she could have everything: the love of the man she loved, children, and a career. That was a pipe dream. The day might indeed come when women could have everything but those days were not yet. Flora Currie has it all, a voice tugged at her as she opened the front door. No, no, she has given up medicine; she has sacrificed her career, her calling, her vocation, for motherhood and now she sits alone while her only child is sent away from her. That is not for me.

Flora Currie, Lady Inchmarnock, was very rarely alone even though her beloved Jamie

60

was at boarding school. Sandy, her husband, her lover, her best of friends, was usually there and if he was not then there were countless visitors, endless committees. Flora sighed as she decided that in many ways this, the third of her three lives, was the least fulfilling.

At first there had been Medicine and for many years she had tried to make it enough for her and, in many ways, it had been enough. There had been too few hours in the day to be a woman doctor at the beginning of the twentieth century. Then there were the joyous years in Australia. Married to her beloved first love, Sandy Fotheringham and, against the odds, mother of their son, she had still been able to practise medicine. Men and women, hundreds of miles from the nearest town, had been more than happy to have a fully qualified doctor on the place, even if the doctor was a woman.

But now?

'You're in your fifties, old girl. Time to be settling down, playing the Society matron.'

'I've never been older than twenty-five in my life, Sandy Fotheringham, *Old Boy*,' teased Flora. 'Besides, why should I slow down when you don't?'

He said the wrong thing. 'I'm a man, darling. It's my duty to carry on.'

Flora stood up and threw her cushion at him. 'If there was such a word as pish-tosh I'd say it. Pish-tosh. Pish-tosh.'

His Lordship retrieved the cushion, hand embroidered – but not by his wife, and returned it to the sofa. 'Flora darling, you have worked all your life.'

'Through choice, Sandy. Doesn't that tell you something?'

'It does, but I hoped having me to look after and then our gift, our boy...'

'Who boards at school,' interrupted Flora. 'This isn't Australia where I was delighted to have one person to help me. Here I have a house keeper and a maid. Good works without real substance are a waste of my talents.'

'Are you not working with Miss Morrison, our first woman prime minister?'

The cushion found itself again on the opposite side of the room.

'Sandy Fotheringham. The woman may well one day be Prime Minister, but she'll do it without any help from me. She's Labour, my dear.'

Sandy picked up the cushion and tucked it under his arm. He went to a sidetable where a tray of glasses and a bottle of sherry stood. Sandy poured two glasses and still with the cushion under his arm he carried a glass to his wife.

'Put the cushion down. You look silly.'

'Inchmarnocks are incapable of looking silly,' said Lord Inchmarnock who now had the cushion balanced on his head.

His wife studiously ignored him.

'I was just going to say that her political party should be no barrier. You're the most Labour person I know.'

'But I couldn't vote for them, darling. Goodness I've done enough in my life to raise family hackles. Helping Elsie Morrison into Parliament would be the last straw. Now tell me about the call from Jamie.'

Sandy replaced the cushion on the sofa, kissed his wife lightly on the cheek, and returned to his own chair. 'He has a new chum, a Mexican child, and he wants to bring him home for tea.'

'Mexican?'

'Yes, strange place, Edinburgh, to send a Mexican child.'

'He's an ex-pat?'

'No. Alejandro Alcantarilla-Medina is pure Mexican. Very good pianist, you'll be happy to hear – keep our little savage on his toes, and they are blood brothers and have sworn eternal friendship.'

He told his wife that their son had been punished for using a knife in the school grounds.

'Good Heavens, I hope they sterilised it.'

'There speaks doctor and mother. If they did not, you may nurse them both this weekend. I've asked permission to have them stay on Saturday night. Jamie also tells me, by the by, that young Medina is the best fighter in the whole lower third.'

'A definite asset to any family,' said Jamie's mother dryly.

She was frowning with concentration. 'Sandy, is Alcantarilla-Medina a famous name in Mexican history? I seem to be familiar with it; almost as if one had learned it at school. In fact I could only have heard it at school. Who has ever heard of Mexico? Do I even know where it is?'

'Below the U.S.,' she answered herself, pushing the question away irritably with her hand. 'But what do I know about Mexico and why is that name familiar?'

No matter how hard she tried Flora could not find the answer to her puzzle. Instead she put her not inconsiderable energy into preparing for her foreign visitor. She decided to treat him exactly as she treated Jamie and therefore what would be needed would be lots of food and lots of hot water, a warm comfortable bed, and a bedtime story.

Sandy went to fetch the boys on Saturday since he, unlike Jamie's devoted mother, was prepared to stand in torrential rain watching his only child play rugby. The boys gave themselves a lick and a promise and then clutching their overnight bags they clambered happily into Lord Inchmarnock's car.

It was Alejandro's first real view of the city where he was to spend so many years and Sandy was familiar enough with the agonies of shy small boys to say 'How do you do?' and then leave him alone to enjoy Jamie's often misinformed commentary.

'And here's Mummy waiting for us,' he said as they drew up outside the Inchmarnock house on Heriot Row. 'Flora, my dear, this is Alejandro who prefers to be known as Xandro, and that's with an X, not an S. Xandro, this is Jamie's mother, Lady Inchmarnock.'

Flora looked down into eyes that she had seen years before and swayed for a moment with shock. She recovered quickly and ushered the boys into the house out of the rain.

'Come along, boys, nice hot baths and then lunch, and then Daddy thought, Jamie, that Xandro might enjoy seeing the castle.'

Jamie made a face. 'If we have to, Mummy,' he said, 'but first I'll show him my room.' He grabbed Xandro's rather grubby hand and pulled him towards the stairs and Flora stood there looking after them.

'Flora, my love, are you ill?'

'No, my dear.' Flora smiled at her husband and watched the lines of worry smooth out on his dear face. 'You will never believe it, Sandy, but I've suddenly remembered where I heard the name Alcantarilla-Medina before.'

Quickly, before the children came back, she told her husband what she remembered.

When she had finished he looked at her, his face a picture of dismay. 'Well, my very dear, how on earth are we going to handle this situation?'

Episode 4

The air was heavy with both grief and threatened rain. Mother Mercedes sat at her desk, her back as straight as it had been the day she said 'goodbye' to young Alejandro, although, unlike the spine, the once beautiful hands were now twisted with advancing age. The face was lined but the eyes were as keen as ever and they bored into the girl who knelt on the floor beside the desk.

'It is unforgivable, Rosaria. I trusted you.'

The girl's head, if that were possible, bent even closer to the floor so that her forehead was almost touching the scrupulously polished wood. 'Lo siento, Madre. I am sorry, Mother. Please forgive me. Such a lapse will not happen again.'

'To the outside this would seem such a small thing, child. You were told to clean the lavatory, and you said that you had done it. You lied.'

'I meant to return. It was just ... the desert looked so lovely, and I watched the setting sun.'

'And enjoyed yourself while someone else did your work.' The old nun sighed. 'I know that to marvel at His creations is to worship God, but to work is also to pray. There is a time for cleaning and a time for wondering at the beauty of the desert in the spring-time.'

She stood up and went to the window. Outside the walls lay the great plain of Mexico, an arid desert most of the year and a riotous feast of flowers for a few days every spring. She would not tell the girl that she sympathised. Duty came first – always.

'Go to the chapel and remain all night prostrate in prayer.'

'Yes, Mother.'

'And you will clean the lavatory every morning and evening until God sees fit to send us a new Novice.'

She turned from the window as the girl, whispering her gratitude, rose and slipped away.

'Were you too hasty, Mercedes? Two years since we last had a Novice. That child will be tired of lavatories long before then. You will have to find some reason to forgive her.'

She went to her desk and her eyes smiled as her hands touched the leather bound cover of the book that lay there. The Novice who was now lying on the cold stone floor of the chapel would have been surprised to see the softness of the look that had replaced the anger that had scalded her.

'Duty, Xandro,' said the nun softly as she opened the book. 'Duty must always come first.'

Inside were pasted all the letters and photographs that she had ever received either from Alejandro Alcantarilla-Medina or from his formidable uncle, Don Alvaro, now dead, God rest his soul.

Not too many photographs but each one a treasure. Xandro was a correspondent though, and he wrote as he talked.

A sepia photograph of a solemn little boy in a smart suit looked up at her. A letter in Don Alvaro's precise handwriting accompanied it.

As you can see, the boy is being cared for devotedly. He will be allowed to contact you but I do ask you never to reveal his whereabouts to anyone.

She turned over a few more pages and saw a large picture of a multi-turreted building; Fettes College, the school in Scotland to which Alejandro had been sent nearly six years ago.

This is where I have my lessons and my meals.

I sleep in another building, a separate house. Scotland is cold and the food is worse than in the orphanage but there are lots of pianos. One belonged to Rachmaninoff. They do not allow me to play it. Jamie says that's silly. He thinks it's just a piano.

She laughed at the postscript. *Don't worry. He really is very nice.*

Another picture. Two very dirty little boys in what she assumed was rugby kit. The boys were almost the same height and Xandro's arm was lying across his fair haired little friend's shoulder.

This is my friend. His name is Jamie. His people have asked me to stay. His mother was a doctor but she does not give people medicine any more and his father is a Lord which is the same but higher than Don. He is nice and says we have the same name.

She turned more pages and more pictures and letters and copies of school reports lay before her.

French – excellent. Mathematics – excellent. English grammar – poor. Behaviour – questionable.

So at least one of these so formally suited masters had a sense of humour. She smiled. Xandro's behaviour had always been questionable but there was no badness in him.

70

One teacher slapped me for playing Rachmaninoff's piano but the music teacher was only angry on the outside – like you sometimes.

Alcantarilla-Medina, he roared. If you are so anxious to play the Maestro's piano, you must learn how to play it properly. You will come to my room every day after luncheon and practise.

So now I have a music lesson every day. I learn Scottish tunes for Lord Sandy and he dances when I play in his house and Lady Sandy laughs and says he is a baby.

Two boys in a rowing boat in the middle of a Scottish loch – laughing, always laughing at the person who took the picture.

This is near Dundee, near Jamie's family home. They do not go there because there was a tragedy. One of the sixth formers called me a wog and Jamie made his nose bleed and was gated for a week so I punched the blighter too and got gated with Jamie. We have vowed to be inseparable. Did I tell you that in our first year we became blood brothers? What funny little boys we must have been.

Thus spoke the old man of seventeen summers. Oh, Xandro, my child, how I miss you.

I miss you and think of you and I say my prayers every night that, one day, I will come

71

home to Mexico and bring Jamie. But I love Scotland too. Even when it was cold and I was lonely, I loved it. Isn't that strange…

The picture she looked at now was of two young men. How quickly they grew. Was it not only a few years ago that La Dama, the sad Lucia Alcantarilla-Medina, had come back to have her unwanted baby in the Convent where she had spent the Civil War years. Lucia had wanted her baby, but not enough to live for it, and Don Alvaro had, in his limited way, cared for his motherless little nephew, but he too was dead, killed in a car accident on a treacherous mountain road. And she, Sister Mercedes, she had cared for Lucia's baby and watched him grow and had then done her duty and allowed the child to be taken from her.

Mother Mercedes never wondered about the child's father. There was a wedding ring, gold encrusted with priceless emeralds, and together with Lucia's jewelled crucifix it remained in the Convent safe. One day they must be given to Alejandro. But in the meantime there was Don Jose Luis.

He was shown into her office and she thought how like his late father he was; handsome, suave, courteous but with the venom of the rattlesnake ready to strike just below that sophisticated veneer. They exchanged exquisite courtesies. She too had been raised by a family that had left its roots in Spain.

'And now, dear sister,' said Don Jose at last, the preliminaries over, 'the time has come to speak of my poor sister's disgrace, about the child she bore here.'

He looked at her but her old eyes merely looked back at him, giving nothing away.

'The boy is named as Alvaro's sole heir; you must know that, Sister.'

'God rest Don Alvaro's soul, Don Jose Luis. I was not privy to the contents of his will.'

'The contents of the will do not concern either of us. I do not need his money and you do not want it. But the child... I must know where the child is.'

So much she could tell him. 'The boy was taken from here many years ago, Senor. I have not seen him since.' Her long fingers lay quietly on the cover of the album. She spoke the truth. She had not seen him.

'But you know where he is.' It was a statement, not a question.

Her answer was polite but ambiguous. 'The Alcantarilla-Medinas of this world do not share their secrets, Don Jose Luis.' She stood up and he was forced to stand up too.

'Sister, the child is of my blood. I have no sons and he is my brother's heir. What anger I had is directed now only to his father, not to the child. I would make amends for the injustice met by the child and by my brother. I loved Alvaro, sister, and I loved my sister. You must believe that.'

'I cannot help you, Senor.'

'Or will not. Good day, Sister.'

He left as abruptly as he had entered and when she was alone she fell to her knees on her Prieu Dieu. Was he sincere? Xandro was Alvaro's heir. Alvaro had been a rich man. Did Jose Luis mean to make sure that the boy inherited the fortune? Did he mean to make him heir to the vast fortunes of his family? Or did he mean to harm him?

I beg you never to disclose his whereabouts to my brother.

That was not in Don Alvaro's will but it was what he had asked of her. Dear God and Father. Make sure that I do what is right by the child. I will not tell.

The years, and her husband, had been good to Nellie Bains Sinclair. She was a contented woman as she sat by the fire sewing, even though her material was rather unwieldy.

Tam, at the close of a long day's hard work, entered his tied cottage, took off his bunnet and scratched his head in perplexity. 'I've seen ye doing some gae daft things, Nellie Sinclair,' he said as he dropped into the well worn chair on his side of the fireplace, 'but can I ask ye why you're sewing a goose.'

Nellie looked up at him and smiled, the same smile that had turned his heart to putty all those years ago. She bent down to bite through the thread, her usual way of cutting, and grinned at him over the goose's neck. 'That daughter of yours – disnae know her own strength. I asked her tae ring this goose for up at the hoos and she took the heid right aff it. Maybe it's her should be the doctor and oor Jimmy, the teacher.'

Tam watched his wife attach the head of the goose – with exquisite little stitches – to the rest of its body. He thought deeply but then realised that he just had to know, 'Nellie, I'm shair this a daft question, by why are ye botherin?'

'No a daft question, Tam. Victoria's got that genteel; it's presentation, that's the favourite word these days, presentation.' She stopped smiling and looked unutterably sad. 'Mistress Menmuir is bringing auld

Davie for his dinner tomorrow. Last winter was hard on him. He's not recovered from that pneumonia he had.'

'Dae ye think...' began ~~Davie~~. TAM

She could not bear to think. 'I don't think, Tam Sinclair,' she snapped, 'and you're no to think either.' Suddenly she jumped up, nearly depositing the goose, now complete with head, on the fireside rug. 'Look, Tam, a letter from Jimmy. Read it for yerself. He's playing football for the university, he's done that well in his last tests, and he thinks he'll be able to get back for the Young Farmers Dance. That'll be a good practice for Andrew's twenty first. Oh, and can we send him a postal order for five shillings, and your mother knitted him some socks, though whit like they'll be I daren't think. Still, it's the thought,' the almost perfect housewife said, 'But you read and find oot for yersel.'

She stopped for breath and Tam smiled and opened the envelope to read the letter just to see his son's words on the paper. If the truth be known he never needed to read anything because Nellie kept him well informed. Still he could not keep himself from teasing. 'Fancy,' he said, 'It says here oor Jimmy's playing football for the university.'

Nellie laughed and carried the goose into the kitchen. She put it into the large roasting pan that was waiting on the table and then she turned the heat up under her soup. Spring, summer, autumn, winter, Tam Sinclair liked his soup.

'Keep an eye on the stove, love, while I'm up at the house.'

Deep in his newspaper, Tam made no reply, but Nellie knew he had heard. She unlatched the door, came back and lifted her pan, and then walked backwards through the door pushing it open with her generous rear. Nellie had no interest in the emaciated fashion models that stared at her from her daughter's fashion magazines. Any one looking at her could tell instantly that Tam Sinclair was a good provider. Mind you, his daughter looked as if she was in dire need of a decent meal and Nellie fumed at the vagaries of fashion. Her employer, Victoria Cameron Wellborn, had two daughters who also looked like some of those starved refugees who were flooding into Britain.

'It's a daft world,' decided Mrs Sinclair. 'Them that's got it dinnae want it.'

'Victoria,' Nellie yelled when she reached the farmhouse. There was no ceremony between mistress and maid. They had been

77

to the same school, Nellie had worn Victoria's cast off clothes – (unfortunately for Nellie, Victoria had stayed slim while she had slowly and inexorably expanded) – they had worked in the same jute mill. Nellie could barely remember those days. They seemed to have been the careers of two other young women.

Victoria came into the hall and led the way into the farmhouse kitchen. The smell of baking permeated the air.

'You're near as good as old Mrs Menmuir,' congratulated Nellie.

'The smell is, Nellie, the tastes are very different. Thank you for doing this. Davie does like roast goose.'

Without being invited, Nellie sat down at the table she had scrubbed only that morning. 'How is he?'

'Oh, I'm worried, Nellie. He's just not pulling out of it. Mother has phoned Lady Flora and they're coming through tomorrow as well. Isn't it funny. They're only in Edinburgh but we see them so seldom. Two rivers to cross really add to the length of a journey and then there's the fact that they've never come back to Inchmarnock and then Mother thinks differently about Lady Flora now that she's Lady Inchmarnock and not her old lodger.'

'Och, Dr Flora's the same as ever she was. She's that good to my Flora, has her to tea at their house though I'm no too happy about that. Jamie – the Honorable James – has been there a few times and Flora likes him. I don't want her getting ideas above her station. We've come that far, Victoria. Can you mind the wee ragamuffin I was afore your mam gave me some clothes and now here's my wee lassie taking tea with a lord's son.'

'He's only a laddie, Nellie. I wouldn't worry and now you'd better get off and feed Tam. They're ploughing tomorrow.'

Nellie stood up. 'Aye, my Tam, Grieve at Priory Farm. I'm that feared sometimes that things'll change, Victoria. I want life to go on like this for ever.'

'And why shouldn't it? Off you go and I'll see you in the morning.'

She waited until the door had closed behind Nellie before she started to deal with the goose. Her mind raced with worry over her Davie's health. What would her mother do if anything happened to Davie? Andrew too, almost twenty-one, still needed a man's guidance although he pretended he was secure. And now Nellie had given her another worry. Flora Sinclair, daughter of her cleaner and a farm worker, was *fond of* the Honourable Jamie Fotheringham. Flora was older than Jamie, her practical side told her. But not by much. He was only a schoolboy and she was already at teacher training college. Perhaps the schoolboy was fascinated by the student's sophistication.

'Oh, Victoria Welborn. How could the daughter of a farm worker be more sophisticated than the son of a lord. Flora's very pretty, mind you.'

Victoria slapped the goose angrily and decided that the problem, if there was a problem, was not hers. She had more than enough of her own.

Andrew Menmuir put the telephone receiver down and did not notice that he had missed the cradle. He felt as if he was choking and rushed to the back door and threw it open. He stood there feverishly gulping in a great drafts of cold damp evening air. Why? Why had he done it? What could he do? How could he turn the clock back? Such a silly little thing, such a stupid... He began to sob, great wrenching sobs.

'Mercy me, Andrew, we will all get our deaths if you keep that door open.'

Miss Davie, his mother's long standing lodger, was behind him, gently pulling him, twice her size and weight, into the kitchen. She closed the door and turned and for a moment the boy looked at her and he was a boy, not a man, and he cried. She held him, muttering soothing sounds while her mind raced. It had to be, it had to be and yet she had hoped and prayed.

'Tell me, dear,' she coaxed.

'They treat me as if I'm five not near twenty-one, Miss Davie. "Come and take your dinner with your sister and her family. They're having a goose. Your father likes a nice goose".'

He was too big for her to hold but she did not want to let him go. 'Andrew dear, I was coming in to make some Ovaltine. I'll make some and you can tell me. It's your father, isn't it.'

He sat down heavily in an old chair. 'Eddie phoned. He's staying with the wee lassies. Lord Inchmarnock has taken Mum and Victoria to the hospital. He's collapsed, Miss Davie. Even Dr Flora couldn't do anything and Dad always said she was the best doctor in the world. He's going to die and I wouldn't even go with him to the farm and he loves it when we're all together.'

81

He sat up rigidly straight for a moment and then with a fiendish howl of anguish, he started to weep again. 'My granny, my granny. She's there too. Oh, God, what am I sitting here for? I need to get to my granny.'

Miss Davie turned to him with the manner that had terrified generations of Classics scholars. She understood more from what he left unsaid and her heart was heavy. 'Andrew, you are no use at all to your mother or to your granny until you are calm. You will drink your Ovaltine and then you will wash your face, comb your hair, and I will drive you to the hospital.'

At the Dundee Royal Infirmary they were told that David Menmuir was in Intensive Care and in a waiting room they found three generations of women who loved him, his mother, his wife and his step daughter. A fourth generation stayed weeping at home in the arms of their father.

Catriona saw the young son who caused her so much anguish and she forgave him everything as she witnessed his very real grief.

'Oh Mum, oh Granny, I'm sorry I didn't come for my dinner. Can I see him? I want to see him.'

Victoria made her brother sit down. She

was very upset and she did not want to scream at him. 'Oh yes, you want him to forgive you.' Instead she made room for him beside her and across from Catriona and old Mrs Menmuir who sat wrapped in grief and in each other's arms.

'It's no richt, Catriona. I should go afore my bairn. I ken he's a man grown and a grandfather but it's no richt.'

'Don't say it,' begged Catriona. 'Not while there's a chance,' and they were quiet.

All five sat staring at the walls thinking their separate thoughts while the hours ticked past and at last Lady Flora Inchmarnock and a young nurse came for Catriona and Davie's mother.

'Would you like to sit with him, Mrs Menmuir? I'm so very sorry but it won't be long now and we thought you would like to be with him.'

Catriona rose slowly and stiffly and gave her hand to her elderly mother-in-law.

Mrs Menmuir looked at Lady Inchmarnock and smiled and Victoria was to remember afterwards that it was a beautiful smile of utter content. 'Och thank you,' said the old lady, but to whom did she speak? 'It jist wouldn't have been richt,' and she slipped slowly to the floor.

Everyone was transfixed with horror. 'Come Catriona, and you too Victoria,' said Lady Inchmarnock. 'I'll take you to Davie. Miss Davie, please take Andrew and get him a cup of tea. Go on, Andrew, my husband's outside. Stay with him, there is nothing you can do here.'

Victoria led her mother away to the ward where Davie was. Like his mother, he looked peaceful. His breathing was slow and shallow and Catriona straightened her back and went to sit beside him. She took one of his frail old hands in hers. Victoria, her heart full of anguish, sat on the other side of the bed and mother and daughter waited for the end.

It was not too long. Davie Menmuir died as he had lived, quietly and with dignity, and Victoria, feeling a hundred years old, put her arms round her mother and led her away.

Outside in the corridor, Miss Davie and Andrew were waiting for them with Lord Inchmarnock, and Andrew went to his mother. 'Come on, Mum, I'll drive you home.' He seemed to have matured quickly. 'Victoria, are you well enough to drive home or will I phone Eddie?'

'I'll bring Miss Davie, Andrew, and I'll ring Eddie from the house.'

Catriona stopped and turned to the Inchmarnocks. 'Go home, old friends,' she said. 'You have a long drive ahead of you and we'll be fine.' She smiled. 'They were both that pleased to see you and hear about wee Jamie. It's been a perfect day. Mother Menmuir would be honoured if you would attend her funeral.'

Flora Sinclair was furious with herself because she was delighted that the Honorable James Fotheringham was to attend the double funeral. Young Flora had known the Menmuirs all her life but there was no close relationship and she was not really unhappy or consumed by grief. Her mother, however, had known Mrs Menmuir well all her life, and she was grieving for herself and for her friend and employer.

Victoria was trying hard to be strong for her mother's sake but she sincerely mourned her stepfather who had given her nothing but love and kindness. Her grief at the loss of Davie's mother went even deeper, for Mrs Menmuir was the last of the old people, the last one on the farm who had known her grandfather, old Jock Cameron, from whom Victoria had eventually inherited her beloved farm.

She wanted to hold the wake at the farmhouse but gave in to Catriona's desire to honour her husband and his mother in the house where both of them had lived for the last twenty years.

Young Flora Sinclair went into Dundee on the morning of the funeral to lend a hand with the preparations.

It was a fine May day and Dundee looked its best. The Tay sparkled in the spring sunshine and gardens were rioting with late spring blossom and early summer flowers. Late daffodils turned their golden heads up towards the glory of early roses and Flora tried hard to make her spirits echo the sadness of the day and not the joyous abandonment of Nature.

She gave up the unequal struggle and almost danced from the bus stop along Blackness Road.

'Mr Menmuir loved flowers. He would be glad that I like them too,' she consoled herself as she reached the house.

A stranger opened the door to her and at first she did not recognise him. He was slightly taller than she was and his hair was the blackest she had ever seen, blue black, like a raven's when the sun hits it.

For a moment they looked at each other

and then the boy spoke.

'Hello, you are Flora. Jamie has told me about you. Please come in.'

Flora smiled. 'You're, how do you say it, Xandro.'

'Very good. Today I am the butler. Jamie will go to the church with his parents but I did not know Mr Menmuir or his mother and have been asked to stay here, and *mind the fort,* I think Lady Sandy said. Mrs Menmuir and her son have already gone somewhere and there are two women in the kitchen.'

'Mrs Welborn asked me to come and help out.'

'I have not met Mrs Welborn although I know who she is. I should not be here but Jamie had asked me for the mid-term holiday and I was quite prepared to remain at school but Lady Sandy said I should come.'

Flora had actually said 'It's as good a time as any,' but Xandro had not read anything into that remark.

'I can tell you're foreign,' said Flora and then blushed with embarrassment but Xandro was unperturbed.

'Because of my skin or because of my English?'

She looked at him candidly. His skin was

87

not white but it was not brown, more a lovely golden colour like a perfect sun tan. 'Your English, really. It's very good but it's...'

'Stilted?'

'I suppose.' Flora thought hard. 'It's as if you're translating.'

'I am – some of the time. I did not learn English until I was ten. My ... guardians thought English was a barbaric language, nothing musical about it.'

Music. Jamie had told her his friend was a musician and a good one. Seemingly he was the only student at the school who had ever been allowed to play a piano belonging to some great composer.

'I must go and help in the kitchen but ... sometime ... I would love to hear you play, Xandro.'

He bowed, a funny old-fashioned little bow. 'I have discovered a very awful piano and I have been playing. For you I will play Mozart and perhaps that will ease your work or your pain if you mourn.'

She knew nothing of music. Piano tunes to ease pain or make work lighter. What a silly idea. She smiled. He really was such a handsome boy; nicer looking than Jamie. It was his eyes. One of Mrs Welborn's wee lassies had eyes almost that colour, like sea water when it runs over stones.

'Mozart would be lovely,' said Flora and went past him into the kitchen.

Xandro went back to the room at the front of the house where he had been told to wait for the Inchmarnocks and sat down at the old upright. The outside had been lovingly polished and dusted but oh, its poor interior workings. He had worked hard and, had there been a musician in the house, they would have known the sound was better than it had been for some time but Xandro had given up on perfection. He sat at the piano because he could not do otherwise and he played because he could not help himself.

For Flora he played Mozart, rippling notes that chased one another in wild but masterly controlled abandon up and down the scales, but when he could no longer tolerate the poor quality of the music he and his instrument were making he stopped and idly turned the pages of the music books that were stacked on top.

Several of Lord Inchmarnock's favourite tunes were there in simple form.

Afton Water
The Rowan Tree

and the one that, for some reason he did not understand, always made Lord Inchmarnock's eyes fill with tears, *Oh, Where, tell me where, is my highland laddie gone.*

Alejandro Alcantarilla-Medina began to play and because he was a musician he re-orchestrated the simple notation he was reading and so created the balm that made the women in the kitchen forget their work and the women who came back to the house from an early visit to the church forget their mourning.

Catriona stood and looked at the boy who sat at Davie's piano stool. She pushed away her daughter's hands when Victoria tried to make her sit down and she leaned against the door and listened to her husband's favourite tunes as he himself had never heard them played.

And then the pianist realised that he was no longer alone in the room and he turned round and, seeing the woman who was, without doubt, his hostess he sprang to his feet and came forward.

'Lo siento, Senora, I mean, I'm so sorry, Madame, forgive my rudeness,' and, for the first time in eighteen years, Catriona looked into her first husband's eyes.

Episode 5

Nellie went in to Draffen's to get some material for a dress for her daughter, Flora. She saw what she wanted right away and, shopping successfully concluded, wondered what to do until her bus came. At first she thought she might pop upstairs to the tearoom, she loved being able to go into a nice restaurant, pull off her gloves slowly, and order a pot of tea and some cakes – and be able to pay for it, not like in the 'good old days.' Nothing good about them. 'Oh, yes,' thought Nellie proudly, 'we Bains have come along way and none farther than Nellie Bains Sinclair with a son at the university and a daughter at a teacher training college.'

Jimmy's graduation came to the forefront of her mind. Truth to tell, it hovered and bubbled deliciously and constantly just under the surface. Resolutely she turned her back on cream cakes. She was not on a diet, didn't believe in that nonsense but no point in adding an ounce or two before the big day.

As befitted a matron with a pound or two in her purse and a son graduating from Medical School, Nellie decided that she should walk along the High Street and look in the shop windows. Perhaps she would see a pair of cuff links – the perfect gift for Dr. (Almost) James Bains Sinclair. What if Jimmy were to hyphenate his names, Dr J. Bains-Sinclair. Had a certain ring to it.

Nellie turned left when she reached the street and, since it was a fine day, she stepped out and soon found herself up the Nethergate, past some of the University buildings, and well on her way to Blackness Road where Catriona Cameron Menmuir lived. Through the glorious spring blossoms she could see fine brass plaques on several of the buildings shining in the sun and she found herself reading them; splendid Scottish names with letters after them, letters that told the world that these men were medical practitioners. Nellie's maternal heart swelled inside her and she thought she might burst with the joy of it.

'My son, the doctor.'

Just think. Jimmy could maybe get a job here in one of these practices. His name, with all those hard won letters after it, would be on a shining plaque for all the world to see. The best people in Dundee would flock to his surgery. 'Aye.' Nellie laughed. 'The *best* folk, his ain folk.'

The poor folk would come and Dr James Bains-Sinclair, (yes, definitely with a hyphen) would be able to treat them because of the money the rich folk would pay him. Not that there weren't some nice folk among the rich. Nellie had met one or two. There were the Inchmarnocks, and Mr Arbuthnott Boatman, the lawyer, he had been a nice man and his son too, and Mr Smart that owned the jute mill. Maybe it was harder to be nice if you were rich but, no matter how hard she tried, Nellie could find no real reason for why this should be so.

A car drew up a few yards ahead of her and a young girl, the same age as her own Flora, stepped out of the driving seat. A slip of a girl driving a car like she was used to it, took it for granted. The changes I have seen in my day, mused Nellie.

What a wonderful world it was and what a great year 1939 was proving to be, if you put aside the deaths of dear Davie Menmuir and his mother.

Ach, she was that close she'd pop in and see Mrs Menmuir. She could give Victoria all the crack of the farm over a cup of tea.

Catriona was a little surprised to see her surprise visitor but pleased too.

'You've just missed Victoria, Nellie. She's away to do some shopping but come in. I'm sure she won't be a minute.'

Nellie's sophistication had left her as soon as she had opened the wrought iron gate that the blacksmith from Priory Farm had made. What a difference there was in this elegant West End property. When the lawyer fellow, Mr Boatman, had bought this place for the then Catriona Cameron it had been a disaster. Broken windows, doors hanging on rusty hinges, gardens wild and over-grown. No one who had not seen the transformation could believe it had ever taken place. But Mrs Menmuir was her own employer's mother and had she not made up parcels of outgrown clothes for the wee lassie who had been Nellie Bains. And here was Nellie inviting herself to call like an equal but if there had ever been inequality Catriona had forgotten it.

'I'm glad to see you, Nellie. Time seems to go so slowly now that I'm alone.'

'And what are you doing in Dundee, Nellie?' asked Catriona after she had made a pot of tea and the two ladies were sitting at a small window table on which one of Catriona's beautifully embroidered cloths had been spread.

The dress material had been shown, patterns considered, and all possible locations for a young doctor's offices discussed before Victoria returned with Miss Davis, the classics teacher who was Catriona's last lodger.

'My you look bonny,' said Nellie for Victoria fairly sparkled.

To Nellie's surprise Victoria blushed. 'Goodness, Nellie, I just had my hair cut; it's been so hot this summer. Do you like it, Mum? I thought I'd surprise Eddie when we go home for the weekend.'

'It would be a surprise,' she thought in anger, and one her husband would not like. She wanted him to be angry, she wanted him ... to what, to show some emotion, to say something besides, 'the west are needs ploughing' or, 'the sheep need dipping.' She wanted, oh, she wanted the Eddie who had loved her on a ship sailing to India, the Eddie who had waltzed with her in the moonlight.

Nellie was looking at her strangely. 'I'll see you on Sunday then, Victoria,' she said as she stood up. 'I just popped in to say hello.'

'It was kind of you, Nellie,' said Catriona sincerely. 'You always were a warm-hearted girl and I'm so pleased about your Jimmy. In fact I'd like to give him his plaque just as soon as you and Tam tell me he needs it.'

Nellie gathered her things together and went off to catch her bus and Victoria and Catriona tidied up and then began to make an evening meal for Miss Davis and Andrew who was expected any minute.

'I like your new hair style, Victoria. The girls will love it but, you never mentioned having your lovely hair cut.'

Victoria turned away and switched on the wireless just in time to hear the end of Deanna Durbin's *One day when we were young*. 'I love that song, don't you, Mum.' She turned back to face Catriona. 'It was an impulse,' she confessed. 'All that heavy hair and day after day of broiling sun. Reminded me of when I was in India and so, instead of passing the salon, I went in and they weren't busy so – off it came. I wonder what Eddie will think.'

We meet and the angels sing poured out of the wireless set and Catriona turned abruptly and switched it off. 'Davie's mother loved that. Goodness it's late and poor Miss Davis ready for her tea. And

Andrew will be home in a minute desperate to eat before he goes out again. He's never in the house five minutes these days.'

'It's his age, Mother. All the young people go dancing. We used to go to socials at the Kirk but nowadays it's dance halls. There's a dance called The Lambeth Walk and a really good one for meeting new girls called The Paul Jones. Even our girls know it. (Victoria spoke as if her daughters were still toddlers instead of grown girls almost finished at school.) Has Andrew taught it to you?'

'Andrew never teaches me anything,' said Catriona sadly. 'But I suppose he'll want all these dances at his birthday party.'

'Of course he will,' said Victoria jauntily in an attempt to cheer up her mother. 'And that's something for you to look forward to.'

Too late she remembered that her brother's birthday and her mother's wedding anniversary were very close to each other. Impulsively she hugged the older woman. 'Davie would have learned the Paul Jones for the party. When we see Eddie and the girls at the weekend we'll talk to them about a wonderful celebration.' She spoke hurriedly, stress in her voice and she did not know whether she was talking to comfort her mother or herself.

'We have so much to be grateful about, Mother. Just look. Those old politicians frightened us with their talk of war and there's to be no war. Chamberlain said so. And Jimmy Sinclair a doctor, and our wee Andrew twenty one years old.'

She dared not yet tell her mother about the man from the garage with the complaint. 'I don't want to worry Mrs Menmuir, but, well, you'd best have it straight, Mrs Wellborn, there's some as says wee Andrew has his hand stuck in the till.'

At Priory Farm all was not well. The hot summer was good for berries and for ripening crops but there was great danger of drought. Such water as was available was given first to the livestock and Eddie constantly had to remind his daughters that they were to save the water, in which they rinsed their hair, for their mother's garden.

'Heavens, Daddy, you'll have us lugging the bath water down the stairs soon,' said Nancy. 'This is Scotland. It rains almost every day – at least twice.'

'If you took your head out of those blasted pony books for a minute, young lady, you would see that this summer is the driest for a long time.'

Nancy and Flora looked at him in surprise. It was so unlike their father to be crotchety.

'Poor Daddy. You're missing Mum. Actually,' teased Nancy, 'It's probably good for you old married men to have to do without your wives for a while. Saves you getting complacent, taking them for granted.'

Eddie smiled. He hated to admit it but there was truth in what his pretty young daughter was saying. He did take Victoria for granted but he would make up for it next year, 1940, the year of their twentieth anniversary. He would take her somewhere wonderful for a second honeymoon: India was too hot but perhaps the east coast of America. It was very pretty there, he had heard.

And then a chill ran through him. War. He was not as convinced as Victoria that there would be no war. He had read the newspapers and listened to broadcasts on the wireless. In March the Czech President had signed away his territory – willingly, it was said, or at least voluntarily. Eddie would be the first to admit that he was not an intellectual man, but he was not stupid and he had been a soldier. To him the annexation of Czechoslovakia was the destruction of the most progressive and democratic state in Central Europe – without a shot being fired. Did that kind of destruction qualify as war?

A few weeks later that man Hitler had demanded bits of Poland. War seemed inevitable. But then the summer, with its long hot halcyon days, had come and there was no more talk of war. The girls were interested only in ponies and tennis, and Victoria had been too occupied with family bereavements to give any thoughts to what was happening across the English Channel.

It was the loss of Davie and his mother that had occupied Victoria's thoughts, that had made her seem so preoccupied lately, so on edge. Or had the discontentment – there, he had said the word – come earlier. Probably, after nearly twenty years of cooking and cleaning, dealing with children and servants, every woman had moments of, what, frustration? There had been her reaction to the church social, so unlike Victoria.

'There must be more to life than church socials and Red Cross sales of work, Eddie.'

Eddie was not frustrated. He had everything that he could ever have dreamed about. A wife whom he loved dearly, two beautiful daughters who gave him no cause for concern, a farm that was the envy of other farmers. Life was good.

Eddie almost shook his head to rid it of unpleasant musings. Nancy was right and he missed Victoria. That was all there was to it.

'Come on, girls, Mummy and Granny will both be here this weekend and this house is really a mess.'

'Nellie's supposed to clean, not us. We have ... piano practice and the horses...'

'And no school until September. Everyone has to help out, girls, while Mummy's away and Nellie's head is busy with Jimmy's graduation.'

'Do you know, Daddy, I think I'll marry Jimmy Sinclair now that he's a doctor,' said fourteen year old Flora. 'He's almost – almost – as handsome as James Stewart.'

'He's got to ask you first, silly little girl,' said Nancy. 'And what Jimmy Sinclair would want with a spotty little girl when he could have...' Nancy stopped. She had been about to say 'me' and the thought shocked her. She had grown up with the Sinclairs. They were friends, their parents worked for her parents, they had just always been there, and who cared if Jimmy had suddenly grown up to look like James Stewart. 'Besides he looks nothing like James Stewart. I'll tidy the kitchen, Daddy, and the living room, but I won't clean the bathroom. Sarah Bernhardt can do that.'

Flora exploded with anger just as her older sister had expected and Eddie tried to quieten them. Oh, please, Victoria, come home soon because girls who are almost women are very difficult. So much easier when horses had been the only animals to interest them.

'Nellie will clean the bathroom. Go and do something about our tea, both of you, now.'

Eddie smiled to himself as the closing door almost caught the hems of his daughters' summer dresses. A little anger was very helpful when you were the type of man who rarely, if ever, exploded. He could hear them talking in the kitchen, united in solidarity against their unreasonable father.

'Please, Victoria, come home soon.'

Victoria reached up to arrange the hair at the back of her neck. Silly. She had had it cut off, a silly spur of the moment gesture just to show Eddie that she was tired of being taken for granted. But she had felt something move against her neck, she just knew she had. Perhaps there was a draught from the open windows. It was so hot, this lovely long summer. The feeling came again and this time she turned. A man, tall, stooping, distinguished, was staring at her and when she turned he coloured faintly and seemed to bow his head in an old fashioned courtly gesture.

Victoria smiled and at this he seemed to take courage.

'I am so sorry to stare, Madame,' he began in very cultured but yet foreign sounding English. 'How can I explain that your neck reminded me...' He stopped and began again. 'Please forgive me. My name is Emil Piaseczany and I am a visiting professor from Poland here at the university. They will assure you that I am not the crazy man who stares all day at ladies whom he does not know.'

What sad, sad eyes. Victoria smiled again and then heard herself speak in a way that she would never have believed possible. 'It's all right, Professor Pias ... Pi...'

'Piaseczany,' he laughed. 'But Emil is more simple.'

'Emil,' said Victoria and knew that she was blushing. 'I felt your eyes. They compelled

103

me to turn.' She blushed again and, feeling a complete and utter idiot, turned away.

'I have embarrassed you, Madame. Forgive me. It was just...'

'That I reminded you of someone.'

'My daughter. She is eighteen and still in Poland and I worry.'

How silly of her to over-react. They were parents, each of them, and each had a daughter of eighteen. She smiled at him. 'Isn't that interesting. You see, I have a daughter of eighteen and one who is fourteen who thinks the horse is the *only* animal worth anything.'

They laughed together.

'Sometimes I agree with her,' said Emil, 'but at other times I remember that if man is what is wrong in the world he is also what is right. I must remember that. You are a lecturer here, Madame?'

'Oh, how I wish I was. I never went to university but one day my daughters will go and I envy them so much. Now the university college here has public lectures and I come whenever I am in Dundee.'

She stopped and they looked at one another and she knew she had to leave – now. 'I only came in to the library. Now I must go.'

He drew himself up in a military way. 'Of course. I have detained you but ... perhaps, Madame ... Madame?'

'Welborn. Victoria Welborn.'

'Madame Welborn, one day we may meet at the public lectures.'

'Perhaps,' said Victoria, and feeling somehow strangely bereft, she turned and walked away. She turned at the door and Professor Emil Piaseczany was looking after her and she half raised her hand before she opened the door and slipped through.

She chided herself all the way down the stairs and all the way to the car park where she had left her car. 'Carrying on like a silly witless girl. Telling a complete stranger – and a foreigner – that you always wanted to go to university. You left that dream behind a life time ago, you silly, silly, middle-aged woman. What on earth were you thinking about? Not enough to do away from the farm, that's your problem.'

She was angry with herself that sad, sad eyes got between her and her sensible thoughts all the way out to Blackness.

She found her mother going through boxes of papers.

'Oh, Mum, why are you worrying about that stuff? I thought we said we'd forget all that legal business for a while.'

Catriona, who was sitting on the fireside rug, looking remarkably young for someone who had passed her sixtieth birthday, looked up when she heard the voice.

'You look relaxed, dear. A little cooler, is it today?'

'No. Yes, it must be. What are you doing, dear?'

Catriona gestured to the rug beside her and Victoria threw her blazer on a chair back and knelt down beside her mother. 'It's that boy, Victoria; Dr Flora's friend. I can't get his face out of my mind.'

Dr Flora's friend? Victoria looked at her mother anxiously. What was she talking about? Was this the beginning of, what senility, decline. No, not Catriona, but still she must be patient, be gentle.

'Don't be silly, Mother. Dr Flora has a son, Jamie.'

'I know that,' said Catriona scornfully as if she had read her daughter's mind. 'I'm talking about the other one, the Mexican boy. In here there's a letter. Do you remember? When we heard that your father was dead – there was a letter from Mexico. I must have kept it. I read it several times.' She bent her head and went back to sorting through the packets of thin airmail letters. 'You sent thin ones and there was ... yes.' Triumphantly she held up an envelope and Victoria took it from her.

'Mother, what on earth has got into you? My father died in some kind of accident twenty years ago.'

'No, not twenty. It was just before you got married. That boy had your father's eyes, Victoria, your father's eyes.'

Victoria put her arms round her mother and pulled her up. 'Mum, you're grieving for Davie. Please, don't put yourself through this. Mexico is a huge country and there must be lots of people with grey-blue eyes. Come on, we should be making the tea. Andrew...'

'Andrew can wait for once.' Catriona pushed herself away, opened the letter and read it through.

'There,' she said. 'There, see it for yourself. Alcantarilla-Medina. That's the boy's name. I knew I had heard it before. He's his son, Victoria. I know it.'

With trembling hands Victoria took the flimsy sheets and read them. 'Coincidence,' she whispered shakily. 'Maybe that name is as common as Cameron here.'

'Nineteen years ago your father was killed,

supposedly by a rattlesnake that got into a house where he was having dinner. That boy is nearly nineteen, Victoria.'

'What difference does that make, Mother? You know he was no good, your first husband, my father. Andrew is living proof of that.' She hesitated. No, she could not yet tell Catriona that perhaps this son was more like his father than they wanted him to be. Hand in the till, hand in the till. No, please, my mother has suffered enough She continued. 'So he went to Mexico and there's another child. It has nothing to do with us, nothing. You owe him – nothing.'

'He's your brother.'

'What are you two saying about me now?'

Victoria turned in relief as she heard Andrew's voice. 'Hello, Andrew. Listeners never hear any good of themselves, young man. I was merely complaining that you don't come out to the farm often enough.'

How easily lies come.

Andrew laughed. 'In these clothes? Tea ready, Mum? I'm going to the pictures with some pals.'

Andrew Menmuir was a well set up young man who could afford to wear the latest fashions. He was elegantly dressed in white flannels and a green and white striped blazer and his shoes were of the softest tooled leather. But against his mother's wishes he had trained as a mechanic and he worked in the garage that Catriona owned in Dundee.

'You didn't go to the garage dressed like that, Andrew?' asked Victoria as Catriona hurried off to the kitchen.

'I'm no longer a mechanic, Victoria. I'm the owner.'

'Not quite, dear. Mother owns the garage.'

'And you own the farm,' snapped Andrew as he sat down.

Victoria looked down at him, her little brother to whom she had given a full half share in the farm she had inherited from her father. Her heart swelled within her as she remembered the early days of his infancy when she had loved him more than anything else in the world. There was Eddie now, and she had her own daughters but she still loved him. Love doesn't turn off and on like a lamp switch even when the loved one shows he is not quite what you wanted him to be.

'Andrew dear. You own half of the farm, you know that, but you have never been interested in farming. I think our father was the same; not interested in putting in, only caring about taking out.'

She hesitated, heard the old cliché, no smoke without fire. Was this the time to ask him about the running of the garage, the garage that Catriona had trusted him to run while she came to grips with two deaths? It was too late. Andrew stood up and glared down at her. 'If you're going to start that *holier than thou,* nonsense, I'm off. Tell Mum I'll get a fish supper and eat it in my car.'

Sadly Victoria went into the kitchen to alert her mother to the news that there would only be the two of them for tea. Miss Davis, Catriona's lodger, had gone to Pitlochry for her usual two weeks holiday.

'I don't know how to get through to him these days. He misses his father.'

Victoria doubted that. Andrew had grown steadily away from both his parents as he had grown older. Wisely Victoria said nothing and merely helped her mother prepare their meal.

'What do you think he'll say when he finds out he has a brother?' Catriona asked into the silence.

'Mother, please. We don't know that and – I don't want to be indelicate – but children whose parents...'

'Illegitimate children, dear,' interrupted

110

Catriona. 'Oh if only we had had the courage to explain his birth to Andrew when he was small, but Davie was adamant that Andrew should always believe that he was his father. It was only when he realised his age that Andrew began to doubt and then when he knew the truth, that your father, my ex-husband, was his father, well he drew away from us, from Davie and me. And now there's another boy, this Mexican boy. Why is he here? What does he want of us?'

'Mother, this is silly. The boy has an unusual colour of eyes; that doesn't make him my brother. And if he is, if, by some wild stretch of the imagination, a Mexican is my brother, half brother, well, what of it. He can't be poor or he wouldn't be at Fettes. That's a really expensive school. The Inchmarnocks chose it instead of Eton for Jamie because they didn't want constant reminders of ... of Lord Inchmarnock's first son, of Robert. Illegitimate children have no rights, Mother. I have no intention of offering a share of my farm to some illegitimate Mexican, so stop worrying.'

Catriona put down her potato peeler and turned to face her daughter. 'I have terrible feelings about this, Victoria. Perhaps it's because I'm still so distressed about losing Davie and his mother but, just think, dear. What if the boy isn't illegitimate?'

Unaware that he was causing so much worry and distress Alejandro Alcantarilla-Medina was enjoying his last summer holiday before entering the London School of Music. He and his school friend, the Honorable Jamie Fotheringham had been in Mexico visiting Xandro's guardians. Because of all the unspoken worries about his family, it had been only Xandro's second visit to his homeland in six years and it was Jamie's first visit and they had loved every minute.

Jamie had loved the sophistication of Mexico City where Xandro's guardian was Director of the Conservatory and he had found himself wondering why Xandro should not study there, in a city and country he loved and with people he loved and who loved him in return.

He asked Professor Himenez if London offered a better education than Mexico City. The old music teacher answered him in French, his second language, since Jamie spoke no Spanish and Senor Himenez no English. 'Bien sur, my Lord. A graduate from London is accepted everywhere. But, you are not a fool, young man, and you are aware that Xandro has secrets in his life. Maybe when you visit Sister Mercedes she will tell you a little but I am sworn to secrecy until Xandro is twenty one. If life was simple Xandro would have stayed with me, been taught by me and not have had to go so far away from the sun. But life is complex, no.'

Aghast, Jamie stared at the elderly man. 'Are you saying Xandro is in some kind of danger?'

Professor Himenez laughed. 'You have seen too many films from our neighbours above the frontera, my boy. Just let me say that when Xandro meets his family, they will meet a man, a fait accompli, not a simple little boy who can be bullied. And if my prayers are answered and it is a world famous pianist who meets the Alcantarilla-Medinas, then ... pouf, it is wonderful.'

When Jamie related this conversation to Xandro, his friend laughed. 'Poor old Tio Himenez. He watches too many American movies. The simple truth is, Jamie, that my mother seems to have forgotten to marry my father and was made to enter a convent, my bachelor uncle left me his share of the family estate, and my other uncle, the head of the family, is ashamed of me and doesn't want anyone to know I exist. Family honour and all that rubbish. You Inchmarnocks should know all about family honour. And don't say a word about my family to my darling Mother Mercedes, she may slap your legs with a ruler.'

Mother Mercedes felt no need to chastise either of the boys. She was happy to see Alejandro and to meet the friend of whom he had written so often and to hear their plans for the future. No, her joy at the expected visit of her son, there she had said it, her son, the child God had given her in her barren virgin state, to love, to nurture, to protect, was immeasurable. She had no right to love him like this, no right to experience this special almost holy love. How many nights had she spent stretched out in abasement on the cold floor in prayer. Yet, she could not conquer this worldly feeling, this love for the child who had lain in her arms, learned his prayers at her knee.

'I am going to study piano and conducting in London, Mother. Tio Himenez seems to think Mexico is too provincial for a star like me,' Xandro teased.

'Perhaps he thinks it better for you to learn to keep your head above water in a very deep pool instead of striding blithely through the shallows.' So easy to sound disapproving. Mothers must scold for their child's well being.

Jamie laughed. 'Gosh, Sister, you sound just like my mother. But Xandro's not really conceited you know. In fact we have to keep telling him how good he is.'

'How good he will be – if he works hard enough,' said Sister Mercedes dryly. 'But enough of Xandro. Is a boy from a family such as yours allowed to make plans, Jamie?'

'Yes and no. I'm going to Sandhurst, our military college. My half-brother, who died before I was born, went there, my father, my grandfather. Had there been a Sandhurst in the Middle Ages Fotheringhams would have toddled along.'

'Jamie would like to learn to fly, Mother.'

The old nun sat back in her straight backed chair. 'Ah. And you feel you cannot ask your father to allow you to break with tradition.'

'It's difficult to explain. My father had a son from his first marriage and he went off, underage, to fight in the Great War. He was horribly wounded and, well, they don't think I know but my Papa's first wife told me that Robert committed suicide. Dad never speaks about him, won't even go near the house where he died, and one day it will be mine and I'll meet lots of old ghosts, I suppose. The fact is that I like pleasing my parents so, Sandhurst it is.'

'You won't know that until you ask them, Jamie. If, as you say, your mother sounds like me, then I would hazard a guess that she is a very practical woman, approachable, yes?'

'Yes.'

'Then tell her you want to fly. In this war that is coming to Europe maybe the birds will be safer than the soldiers.'

The boys looked at her in awe. At school the conversation had all been of the possibilities of conflict. Lord Inchmarnock was sure that the lessons taught by the Great War had been learned and there would not be, could not be another war. Xandro preferred not to think about war at all. He was Mexican and had nothing to do with conflict in Europe but his friends, especially Jamie, would all be involved. He took refuge in music. But here in a convent in the middle of Mexico an elderly nun was saying that war was coming.

There was a knock on the door and a nun entered with a tray. Jamie jumped up to take it from her and, embarrassed, she showed him where to put his burden.

'Churros, with sugar,' said Xandro ecstatically, 'and hot chocolate. Jamie is becoming very fond of churros, Mother. He will be too fat to fly if we stay in Mexico much longer.'

Sister Mercedes smiled as she watched the young men with their healthy appetites empty the plate of the sweet pastries. Then she slapped her hands together as if she had come to a decision. 'I have some things I have been saving for you, Xandro. They belonged to your mother. Perhaps it will be many years before you can return to your own country and I, well, I am getting older and who knows.'

She went to her desk, opened a locked drawer and took out a small packet which she handed the boy.

Xandro took the packet but before he opened it he looked at the nun and tried to see what was hiding in her eyes. He felt that he dared not open the parcel; he did not want to know what it contained. He knew that everything would be changed once it was opened and he wanted things to stay the same. She refused to raise her eyes.

Slowly Alejandro peeled back papers whose folds told their age. First he un-covered an exquisite crucifix studied with precious stones and then a ring, a heavy gold ring studded with emeralds. Even his young untutored eyes knew that they were of immense value. His eyes filled with tears. 'Dear little Mother,' he smiled through his tears, 'if these belonged to my mother, why did you not sell them to pay for my upkeep.'

Mother Mercedes fought to remain stoical, practical. 'Your uncle Alvaro was always generous to the whole establishment, nino. We did not need to take your mother's wedding ring.'

The boys stared at her and slowly, reverently Xandro took the ring from the cloth where it had lain for nearly nineteen years. 'Her wedding ring?' he asked and the nun nodded.

'Good lord, Xandro, if there is a wedding ring there must have been a husband. Seems as if you are all legal and above board, amigo,' laughed Jamie. His young laugh shattered the sleepy silence of the room and made dust motes dance in the heavy air. 'Where is his missing papa, Sister?'

'He died before Xandro was born and

who he was, I do not know. Alvaro knew and he is dead. Better to forget everything, Alejandro. Go to London. Become a great pianist and play for my Lucia, your beautiful mother.'

Xandro dashed his hand across his eyes, perhaps to wipe away tears, perhaps to ward off thoughts.

'My uncle was Don Alvaro Alcantarilla-Medina. My mother was Lucia Alcantarilla-Medina, his sister. I must find out – who was my father and what is my name?'

Early one Sunday morning, Elsie telephoned Victoria from London and was surprised to hear that she was still living with her mother in Dundee. She rang her there.

'Having a high old time away from your husband, are you?' she tried to joke and she could not see that Victoria blushed unbecomingly.

'Don't be silly, Elsie. Mother needs me and Eddie doesn't. Now, tell me about London, Parliament, all that madly exciting life of yours.'

'Victoria, I don't know when I'll be home again. Will you look after my flat for me?'

Victoria sat down abruptly on a chair

119

beside the telephone table. 'Elsie, what are you telling me?'

'Nothing that the whole world doesn't know. Hitler has invaded Poland. I imagine that since my parliamentary work involves meetings with Defence Department officials, I'll be kept rather busy here. You have keys to the flat?'

'Yes.'

'Then give it an airing now and again, whenever you're in town.'

When the conversation was completed Victoria sat on in the chair and she did not think of her husband or her daughters. She thought of the sad eyes of Professor Emil Piaseczany. She had just happened to meet him again at a lecture and he had told her of the life in Lodz, his village near Warsaw. Emil saw war as inevitable.

'I should have returned earlier,' he had said. 'The Polish cavalry is the finest in the world. I should have joined the army and kept this monster out of Poland.'

'On a horse? Emil, Hitler uses tanks.'

She sat now and heard her voice mouthing platitudes. 'He won't be allowed to go farther. Britain won't allow it. This is 1939, not 1919. Sanity will prevail.'

'Who was that, dear? Eddie?'

Victoria smiled at her mother who was dressed for Church. 'It was Elsie, Mother. Give me two seconds and I'll get my hat.'

Catriona had forgotten the telephone call by the time they returned but she remembered it again later when a wireless broadcast was interrupted so that the King could speak to the Nation. They sat at the kitchen table and listened and at some point Catriona reached for her daughter's hand. It had come.

Britain was at war with Germany.

Episode 6

Lord Inchmarnock had known of the inevitability of a second war but, like many others, he had tried to pretend it would not happen. He looked at the pictures on the desk of his Edinburgh study but could focus on only one of them, his son Robert.

'Never again. It must not happen again,' he said to the smiling young face, the face that had never grown any older.

'I've brought some coffee, darling,' came the voice of his beloved second wife, Flora, and he turned to take the tray from her hands, fussing as he did so that she should not be carrying trays when they paid young Annie to do it.

And Flora who had known exactly how to get her husband's mind off his fears, even for a moment, allowed him to fuss.

She poured coffee into fine china cups and buttered him a scone.

'Just think what Catriona Menmuir would say if she could see you eating a scone I had baked.'

'Well, it's not my eating it, darling girl, it's you baking it that would surprise her.'

They laughed and Fiona thought fondly of her former landlady who had looked after her so well while she had been in practice in Dundee all those years ago. She sighed and wished she had not for instantly he was anxious.

'What is it, Flora, something about the Menmuirs or the Wellborns, or is it our Jamie?'

Flora looked at the pictures on the desk. 'Actually ... oh, don't be cross, darling, but I was thinking about my days in medical practice. Even when we farmed in Australia I was able to be of use. Now that Jamie is grown up, I have so much time.'

Lord Inchmarnock reached for the jam and spread it liberally on the scone.

'Is that to disguise the taste?' she teased and he smiled because circumstances had turned the one time debutante into a ... what could he say ... reasonably good baker.

'He's not adult yet,' he said and, despite himself looked again at the beautiful face in the silver frame.

'He's older than Robert was when he died, darling.'

Sandy Inchmarnock stood up abruptly. 'Died? Killed himself, because of what he suffered in that bloody war. It's not going to happen again. I won't let it.' He reached for his wife and held her close but it was to give himself comfort. 'He's babbling on about the Air Force, our Jamie. Thinks it's exciting, just...'

He could not continue and she held him until he was in control again.

'He won't enlist, Sandy. He knows it would break your heart, but if there's conscription—'

'Time enough to worry about that if it comes to it, damn politicians. Where is he today?'

'Gone up to Thin's to get his books for University.'

He smiled. 'Good, just what he should be doing at his age.' He went over to the fire and put a log on the dying embers and instantly the dry wood sent a shower of sparks racing up the chimney. While his back was to his wife he added, 'I had a visit from old Pringle this morning, Flora, about the house.'

She waited. It was not this house, the house in Edinburgh's lovely New Town that they had chosen together, but Inchmarnock House, the stately home in Fife that he had not visited since Robert's funeral.

'Pringle says some Boffins have been pestering him; they've been going around looking for places to requisition. Can't say I want Civil Servants running all over it but, the thing is...' He could not continue.

'You feel you ought to discuss the Estate with Jamie,' she said calmly as she poured more tea. Dear God, what should we do without our afternoon tea, for as I pour I can try to pretend that I am not terrified about the future of my son, my darling Jamie. Flora smiled at her husband. 'Jamie will inherit one day, darling, you're right, and it would be sensible to talk to him – even to visit the house,' she added bravely.

'No, that I can't do,' he said.

The trees were beginning to turn. Victoria liked to watch them every day, wondering at the speed with which they changed colour, at the way it seemed that some trees started to go yellow on their top most branches and then the autumn colours worked progressively down.

The fields were bare of crops but in some of them fires burned as the farmers prepared for winter and next spring's sowing.

Next spring. Victoria sighed. Where would they be next spring. For the first time in her twenty years of marriage she thanked God for not having granted her the blessing of a son. From her comfortable living room she looked down at the cottage where the Sinclairs lived. Smoke curled lazily from the chimney pots but smoke was the only thing that was lazy about the Sinclairs.

Inside Nellie would be weeping and wailing and berating poor Tam and Chamberlain and Hitler and even God that this war should have come just when her son had become, to his mother's everlasting pride, Doctor James Bains Sinclair, even though the said son refused to hyphenate his two surnames, no matter how his mother begged.

And she who had no son to offer to the war machine was worrying, not about her brother, Andrew, who would certainly be called up, or Jimmy Sinclair who might be, but about Emil Piaseczany who had been unable to eat or drink or sleep since the news had come that Poland had been invaded.

She had met the visiting Polish professor once or twice at lectures at the university. Was it the impending war that had made them friends so quickly? Surely friendships had taken so much longer to form in the old days?

'Or was it that Emil talks to me as if he sees an attractive intelligent woman where Eddie, if he sees me at all, sees only "my wife" and the girls see only "Mother." They don't see *me*, don't seem to care about what I feel or think. Are they aware that I can think? Emil assumed I was on the faculty and oh, what a dream that would have been. And now he is terrified about his daughter and I am the only person to whom he talks freely.'

Victoria turned from her contemplation of her farm, her mind made up. She was going to that lecture at the university and Eddie could say what he liked.

'Be very careful driving back,' was all Eddie did say.

He wanted to say more. He wanted to ask her why she was so withdrawn lately, since Davie Menmuir's death really. He wanted to ask her what he had done wrong for he must surely have done something. But he said nothing, thinking that was the best thing and of course it would have been better to have challenged her. Victoria wanted to fight, to have him show that he cared that she was spending so much time with her mother instead of at the farm – and during the harvest too when a farmer's wife was so vitally needed.

He knew that, although she never said a word to her mother, she regretted that she had been unable, like her friend Elsie, to go to university. Wasn't that why she pushed their daughters and had pushed Andrew, her brother? These lectures the university was sponsoring were a good outlet for her and at first she had come back from them full of facts that she spilled out to him at the breakfast table or even in bed if he was still awake when she drove home. But lately she told him nothing. So:

'Be very careful driving back,' he said as he waved her off.

'If the light's bad I'll stay with my mother,' she answered as she swept, almost in relief, through the farm gates.

She had been staying with Catriona at least once a week since the double funeral but surely, thought poor Eddie, Catriona who had always seemed a very strong woman, should have come to terms with her loss by now.

Victoria saw him standing forlornly by the gate as she looked in the rear view mirror and, for a moment, all her love of him came flooding back. He was such a good husband, such a good man, and he had taken her father's little farm and set it back on its feet; one of the most prosperous farms in the area now and most of that due to Eddie's hard work and intelligence. It was he who had brought in fat sheep to graze the hills where nothing good would grow and he who had added to their cash crop of soft fruits in the few short summer months. If only he could talk of something else beside yields and potato prices and the ridiculous cost of wintering.

She parked down by the river and walked up to the university buildings. Eddie would be cross if he knew she walked so far in the darkened streets but she loved to look at the lights on the river. On a night like this even the moon gazed at its own reflection in the still waters of the Tay and, as always when her heart was troubled, Victoria took comfort from the sight and sound of running water.

Street lights told her that the trees here too were already wearing their autumn colours and she knew that next time she visited the town, the trees would be bare. Just one wild wind rushing down from the Angus glens would strip every leaf from every tree to send them skirling down the streets.

In spite of – or perhaps because of – the outbreak of war, the lecture room was crowded and Victoria found herself a seat at the back. She looked around; this was the fourth of the public lectures she had attended and so she was getting to know some of the others who came regularly. She was not looking for anyone in particular, of course she was not.

He was not coming. The lights were being darkened and so the lecture – she could not even remember the subject or the title – was about to start.

Then he slipped in to the seat beside her.

'I was not coming,' he said, 'but I could not stay away.'

She turned to look at him and wondered at the behaviour of her heart. How silly, how stupid, to be behaving like one of her own daughters, like young Flora when Jimmy Sinclair was home for a weekend. 'Is there any news?'

'It is a shambles. Moscow has announced the partition, the fourth partition of Poland, and the Government has fled to Romania. Dear God, what good will they do in Romania? And I can get no news of my daughter.'

Victoria stood up. 'We can't talk here, my dear. Come, we'll have a cup of tea somewhere.'

Like an obedient child he followed her and then Victoria realised that it was seven-thirty on an October evening. Where on earth could they go for tea?

'Emil, I'm sorry,' she said as they reached the front door. 'I really don't know...' She stopped as an idea came into her head. No, it was insane. She was married and so was he, was he not? They could not... She looked at him. He was a man in a foreign country whose own country had just been divided between Germany and Russia and somewhere in that insanity was his daughter.

'Emil, I hope you don't mind but I can't

think of any tea room which will still be open. However, I have a friend who works in London and I was supposed to go and air her flat. We could go there for a little while. I doubt that you would take in much of the lecture.'

He looked at her and for a moment she saw the imagined horrors in his beautiful dark eyes and then he tried to smile. 'I do not wish to compromise you, my dear Victoria. Your husband would be rightfully distressed to think of you alone with a strange man and a foreigner.'

'Goodness, Eddie has more sense than that, Emil.' She could go to her mother but she stifled that thought. Emil needed to talk, to unwind. With Catriona he would hide all his worries and they would only dig deeper into his soul.

Her mind was made up.

'I promised Elsie I would air the flat and I haven't been in town this week ... so much to do on the farm. It's only a step.'

'If you are sure.'

They walked without speaking up the Perth Road and when they reached Windsor Street Victoria found Elsie's keys at the bottom of her handbag. How embarrassing if they had still been at Priory Farm.

'I'll open the windows and put the fire on,' she said brusquely. 'It's stuffy and chilly at the same time, isn't it?'

'You are ill at ease, dear Madame. I will go.'

'Good heavens, Emil, how silly. We are having a cup of tea. I'll be right back. You turn on the fire and make yourself at home.'

When she came back from the kitchen with a tray he was sitting at the window looking out at the street.

'Soon we will have to close the curtains and turn off all the lights,' he said sadly. 'Do you remember the last war, Victoria, and how we said we would never let it happen again?'

'I was fourteen when war was declared. You?'

'Twenty-four and just finished my doctorate. The boys with even finer minds who died beside me... Dear God, when will we learn?'

She poured some tea and he drank it gratefully.

'Have you eaten at all today?'

'Eaten? My little girl. I wanted to bring her with me but she is in love. *Oh, Papa, I can't leave Ivan for six whole months. I would die away from him.* Perhaps she will die with

132

him,' he said and his voice broke. 'I'm sorry. Forgive me.'

'No, Emil, no. You mustn't think that. The armies won't make war on children. You'll hear from her soon and perhaps she'll come to live with you now. Goodness I'm sure we can find somewhere for you both to live. Here, perhaps. My friend works in the Government. I doubt she'll come home while this war is raging. Everything will be alright. I'll ring her tomorrow.'

He put his cup and saucer down. And stood up. 'You are too kind, Victoria, but I have stayed long enough. We will wash the cups and return to the university.'

'She'll be fine, Emil.'

He looked down at her and she saw that his eyes were full of unshed tears and that he was trying desperately hard to control his emotions. Instinctively she reacted. She held out her arms and, for a second he stood, and then he clutched her to him.

She put her arms around him and then any thought that she was merely comforting a friend in distress was driven away by the pounding of her heart and the racing of the blood around her body.

'Dear God in Heaven, what am I doing?' Emil almost pushed her away. He pulled himself together and gave her a funny old fashioned little bow. 'Please forgive me, it was just...'

'It's all right, Emil. Nothing happened. An ... embrace between friends, no more.'

'Of course, of course,' he muttered. 'Human contact ... we all need. Please, Madame, we will wash the dishes and return ... no, the lecture will be over soon.'

Be natural, Victoria. Instinct warned her.

'Do you want to tell me a little about your daughter, Anneliese, isn't it?' she asked as lightly as possible as she carried the cups back into the kitchen.

'Anneliese, yes,' he said and he smiled as he remembered his daughter. 'She is the image of her mother and turns me around the fingers as her mother used to do. She is going to become a doctor...'

He stopped, unable to continue.

'How wonderful,' said Victoria quickly. 'My mother had a lady doctor live with us when I was a young girl. She was wonderful, an aristocrat who turned her back on her family to study medicine. You must meet her sometime and you can tell her all about Anneliese. It's wonderful what young women are encouraged to study nowadays, isn't it?'

He was not listening. His eyes were bleak as he looked down at her. 'You do not understand, Victoria, here in this wonderful country. I must find some way to get back to Poland. My daughter is a Jew.'

'I'm calling the polis, Mrs Menmuir. This isn't the first time. I talked to him and he said he's been a bit short and meant to put it back in and he did when I said I was coming up here. *My mother has enough on her plate mourning my father and my granny,* he says to me, *It was only a wee oversight, Pete,* says he. But this time it's no a wee oversight, Mrs Menmuir. There's near two thousand pounds missing this month.'

Catriona looked at the honest troubled face of Pete Smith, the manager of Menmuir's Motors.

'I won't say you're wrong, Pete. How often...'

He twisted on the grossly over stuffed chair as if he preferred the negative comfort of the wooden seat in his office. 'You want it straight. You've aye been the straightest woman I know. Straight – it happens every time he's in the office, a quid here, a tenner there, but this is grand larceny. And it's no jist money; there's parts go missing. There's a war on, Mrs Menmuir and fortunes to be made and we can make one honest – but no if your own son is robbing you blind.'

She winced. 'Two thousand you said, Pete. I'll write a cheque but I want you to let me handle it, just this one time. I assure you it won't happen again.'

He sat there watching her write and he could not help himself, it burst out. 'How any man that's the son of Davie Menmuir, as fine a man as ever drew breath could lower hissel to this.'

He stood up and took the slip of paper from her trembling hand and he could not bear the trembling. 'This once, Mistress, but for his sake as well as yours, I'll bring in the polis if it happens again.'

She let him out and went back into the lounge and sank into a chair as if she had suddenly grown stones heavier.

'That's the rub, Pete,' she said. 'He is no son of David Menmuir.'

Catriona sat on for several hours in the room where, so many years before, she had stayed after her encounter with John Cameron, her first husband and Andrew's father. Miss Davie had come in and offered to make a pot of tea and Catriona had roused herself to offer to prepare supper for the woman who had become more a companion than a boarder. Pretending she was still running a boarding house had really been for old Mrs Menmuir's sake, to make her feel that she was still useful. These days Miss Davie drifted in and out, perfectly happy, so she said, to be just one of the family and able to fend for herself.

Catriona looked round. Nothing in the room reminded her of John Cameron; everything spoke loudly of the taste of her dear Davie. Even the fireplace had changed, the old marble one taken out and replaced by a nice modern one. Victoria had taken the old one and put it in a cottage at Priory Farm.

Catriona smiled as she thought of her daughter. Never ever had Victoria given her cause for concern and yet she too was John Cameron's daughter. Catriona brushed escaping hairs from her eyes. It was difficult for her to understand, why one child could be so good and the other so... No, she could not say it; not so good was as strong as she could be.

At last she heard the front door open and her son's steps on the stairs. She pulled herself up quickly and hurried out into the hall. Andrew stopped halfway up the stairs and turned, in surprise, to look at her.

'Hello, Mum, you should be in your bed, an old lady like you.'

Oh, he had his father's charm alright and his looks, although the eyes were more her colour than those amazing sea blue eyes that Victoria and that other boy, the Mexican, had inherited.

She did not smile. 'Come down here, Andrew. I want to talk to you.'

'Too late to chat tonight, Mum. You should be in your bed, and I need my beauty sleep if I want to do a good day's work tomorrow.'

'Have you ever done a good day's work, Andrew?' she forced herself to say. 'Come down now, or tomorrow I will ring Mr Boatman and change my will.'

For a moment he stood defiantly on the stair and then he capitulated and ran lightly down towards her. 'Something's got you in a right mood.'

She recoiled from the smell of alcohol on his breath. Not that he drank much: Andrew always liked to be in complete control of himself.

'Mr Smith was here this afternoon,' she said as soon as the lounge door closed behind them and she was pleased to see him flush and look embarrassed.

At least he did not try to pretend innocence. He was not like John in that regard.

'Temporary embarrassment, Mum. It won't happen again if you bail me out this time.'

'Gambling?'

He took a turn up and down the length of the room and she could almost feel her heart breaking as she watched him, so tall, so handsome, so full of withered promise.

He looked at her as if trying to judge just how much to say.

'Pete wanted to ring the police, Andrew.'

'Don't be absurd, Mother. I can't be arrested for borrowing what is mine.'

'The garage belongs to me and when I am gone, Andrew, half will belong to you and half to Victoria.'

'Your precious Victoria. The farm should have been mine.'

She did not remind him that Victoria had signed over half the farm – to which he had no legal right – to him, at the expense of her own daughters.

'Was it gambling?'

He sat down opposite her and put his head in his hands. A silly empty-headed girl

139

would find him unbelievably attractive, thought his mother.

'More of a sure thing, Mum, a business venture, long term. It's the war. You're so careful and steady, you can't see that there's fortunes to be made out of this war and I ... we might as well be the ones to make them.'

'Camerons and Menmuirs,' said Catriona, mentally casting her first husband out of that group of fine men, 'have never made money out of the misfortunes of others.'

'That's plain stupid,' he said angrily and stood up as if to go.

'Sit down, Andrew, and I will tell you what you will do to redeem yourself. Sit down.'

It had been years since she had spoken to him like that and he sat down and looked at her, his face full of bravura.

'I saw a poster in the town this morning, Andrew, something about the army will make a man of you. It will make a man of you, Andrew, starting tomorrow morning, or you will find yourself in jail and penniless.'

He looked at her and laughed and she sat pressing her fingernails into the palms of her hands to stop herself sobbing, *Mummy doesn't mean it,* and clutching him to her.

'You're joking,' he said. And then, 'You're

not joking. You want me to answer my country's call as they say.'

He stood for a moment looking down at her and then his face crumpled and he threw himself on the carpet at her feet and buried his face in her lap. 'No, Mum, please, I won't do it again. First thing tomorrow I'll apologise to Pete and I'll pay it back. I promise, Mum.'

Tentatively her hands reached out to touch his curling black hair and then she put her hands behind her. 'Tomorrow morning, Andrew, you will enlist and no-one need ever know we have had this conversation.'

She sat motionless and he stopped sobbing and stood up. 'You bitch,' he said at last and ran from the room.

She sat listening to his thudding feet on the stairs and the slam of his bedroom door and only then did she give in to the pain that was tearing her apart. She crouched on the settee and rocked herself moaning and sobbing until the early hours of the morning.

Then she rose stiffly and walked quietly across the room to the door.

'I've always hated this room,' she said as she looked around and then her eyes fell on

141

Davie's piano and she smiled sadly.

'No, never when you were in it, my dearest love.'

'You know, Nellie, noo that I come to think on it, I've never really liked Brussels Sprouts,' said Tam Sinclair as he pulled some nice fat sprouts off the stalks and tossed them into her basket.

Nellie looked at her husband as he stood in the muddy patch that was their garden and decided that she would give him a good dose of salts when she got him indoors. Cured everything, salts did.

'It's bit late tae tell me noo, Tam. I've been cooking them for...' she did some amazing mental arithmetic and was unhappy with her answer, '...near twenty five years for you and if you take aff the years you were away, twenty two years, give or take, well, that's an affie Brussels Sprouts. And you're no jist eating them, Tam Sinclair, you're growing them. You've wasted yer hael life, growing and eating Brussels Sprouts.'

He snorted with laughter as she had intended him to do. 'My life's no been wasted, Nellie,' he said with a gleam in his eye that had her picking up her basket and backing off.

'Away ye go, ye daft auld man.'

Tam stuck his spade into the ground and chased her. 'Auld man, am I? I'll show you who's an auld man, Nellie Bains Sinclair.'

Dr James Bains Sinclair – without a hyphen – heard the laughter of his parents as he walked up the farm track and smiled. What a pair they were. He wouldn't trade them for anyone.

'Behave yourselves you two,' he shouted as he got to the path through the garden. 'I'm a doctor and I have a reputation to keep up.'

'Jimmy,' yelled his mother at the top of her voice though he was barely twenty feet from her and his father smiled at him. 'We wisnae expecting you.'

'Dad was,' said Jimmy and Nellie looked at her two men and felt a cold hand grasp her heart.

'Come ben and get your tea, Jimmy. Yer dad's jist picked us some nice Brussels Sprouts.'

Nellie went on into the kitchen with her basket and Jimmy stayed at the door while his father pulled off his boots. He could never remember his father walking into their cottage with his shoes on, no matter what the weather.

'You've made up your mind, lad?'

'Aye, Dad.'

'Then there's nae mair tae be said.'

Jimmy pulled his father back as he went to walk into the house. 'I want you to be pleased, Dad. I want you to understand.'

Tam looked at his son and remembered a wee laddie playing with kittens on the carpet. He had believed then that this day and what was going to be said was impossible.

'I cannae be pleased, laddie, and I'm trying desperate tae understand. Noo, no another word till ye've had yer tea.'

Jimmy smiled. His mother might treat him like some magical being, Doctor James Bains Sinclair but, thank God, his father saw only his son.

While Tam changed out of his muddy trousers and washed his hands, Jimmy went into the kitchen to help his mother.

'Away ye go,' she said happily, 'Doctors shouldnae be setting tables. Yer dad'll do it when he's changed his breeks, bringing all that mud intae my clean hoos.'

Jimmy looked round. He had always lived in a clean home with a mother who spent her days cleaning and cooking and washing and usually singing, very badly, as she did so. Now that he was older and was qualified, and had seen some of the poorer areas of Dundee, he realised how hard his mother had always worked to keep them all clean.

It was Nellie's spirit that thrilled him. Nothing ever got the better of his mother, not poverty or illness, or a man at the Front. He dropped his eyes. Was he about to deal the blow that would quench her spirit?

He took down the plates and bowls from the kitchen cupboard in spite of his mother's orders and laid them out on the scrubbed table and Nellie worked happily around him muttering things about boys who didn't know their place and doctors who did and getting herself thoroughly mixed up.

Jimmy managed to keep quiet until the bowls were full of good home cooked broth and then he had to speak. 'Mum, Dad, I want to join the Army Medical Corps.'

Tam had not started his soup but Nellie sat, her spoon halfway between her plate and her mouth, and looked at her son.

'The whit?' she finally gasped as the soup splashed on the table.

'The army needs doctors, Mum, and, Dad, I know I won't be called up for a while yet but if I go now I've a chance of going where I want to be and learning skills that

145

will be really good in the future.'

'We've jist hung the nice plate Mrs Menmuir had made, Jimmy,' said Nellie. 'I was planning on cleaning it once a week when I was in Dundee. That lassie that cleans out your offices never kneels down to clean.'

The plaque was at eye level but Jimmy knew what his mother meant. Only women who got down on the floor to scrub could confidently be called decent housewives. Mrs Thomson did not kneel down to tackle dirt; therefore she was an inferior housekeeper. His heart swelled with love for his feisty little mother.

'You can still clean it while I'm away, Mum. Dr Rogers will keep my place. He says he wishes he was free enough to go.'

'Oh, he does, does he,' said Nellie her face beginning to get redder with anger. 'Your dad went tae the last war, the one that was supposed to be the last war and so this family's done its bit. They'll no call up doctors, Jimmy. It would hae tae be awful bad for them to need doctors.'

She realised what she had said, burst into tears, threw her apron up over her face and ran out of the room. Jimmy went to follow her but his father stopped him with a hand that was like an iron vice.

146

'Women are a' the better for a good greet, Jimmy. Leave her be, laddie and eat your soup.'

'I can't.'

Tam pointed with a dirt ingrained finger at the soup bowl and Dr James Bains Sinclair sat down and began to eat.

'She'll come oot when she gets her mind on maybe you're sterving tae death.'

Tam was right and they were only just beginning their second bowl of Nellie's soup when the bedroom door opened and, with red face and swollen eyes, Nellie came back.

'No finished your soup yet?' she began.

'Sit doon, lassie, and let the boy speak. It's no the braw uniform that's making ye think on this, Jimmy.'

'Well, our Flora was mooning over some actor in uniform last week when I saw her, Dad,' teased Jimmy. 'A chap's got to think of everything.'

A chap. Nellie and Tam looked at one another across the table. *All our own work*, was what their delighted eyes said to one another.

'I'll no insult you by telling you there's no glory in warfare, Jimmy, no beauty, precious little honour. War is Hell, lad, and this one will be worse than the last with bombs falling from the skies and exploding out of the depths of the sea. With all them brains, could clever folk no think on better things tae make than guns?'

'I think that's what makes men higher than the animals, Dad. Good men keep thinking we should be doing better, fine men like you.'

Tam laughed. 'Fine men like me? I've nae book learning, laddie.'

'And what a man you would have been with it,' thought Jimmy to himself. 'Education doesn't make a man, Dad,' he said, 'and you've worked day and night to put me through the university and I'm grateful and I want you always to be as proud as the day you saw me walk up to get my degree. Men are going to be hurt, Mum. I can help. I want to help. I need to help. Will you let me go, Mum, and promise to save your lovely hat to meet me at Dundee when I come home. I want to look out of the train and say, "See that woman in the gorgeous hat, that's my mum."'

Nellie thought of the hat reposing in its bag on top of the wardrobe. She had thought never to wear it again because her daughter, Flora, cheeky young miss, had said it looked like a cabbage on her head.

'Course I'll save it and I'll have a good meal ready, Jimmy, for whenever you want it.'

He could not do it, he could not. Memories called to him, horrible, frightening, dreadful memories; a beautiful maimed boy and a gun. No, he could not go back.

'Gosh, Daddy, what an absolutely lovely house,' the excited voice of his living son woke him from his nightmare and he tried to smile.

'Yes, old chap, been in the family for ever but...'

'I understand. Mum told me about Robert years ago. I can understand why you could never come back but it's beautiful and full of all the family history, Dad, not just that one terrible episode.'

Sandy was so angry that he drew back his hand as if to hit his son. One terrible episode. His beautiful son, Robert, had shot himself in the study of that house because he could not live with his disability, and Jamie disposed of it as *one terrible episode.*

Flora's hand was on his arm and he relaxed. The boy was right, of course, as the young so often were.

'I'll show Jamie the house, darling, if you

149

go through the policies and see about the trees. I'm not sure the factor has really been doing a good job.

Darling Flora, giving him a way out. He walked off down one of the woodland walks, hearing his younger son's happy voice chattering to his mother as they drew farther away.

He walked to the duck pond.

'Sensible ducks,' he said when he saw the water flat and shining and completely empty, at least of ducks. 'Too cold by half.'

The holly was bright with berries. 'Why, that tree was always a good source of berries and it still is.'

'Why do the birds strip one tree and not the others, Daddy,' he could almost hear the echoes of a loved voice and, his eyes misty, see the figure of a small figure in a sailor suit.

'Why do some ducks have green heads and some not?' the memory asked him.

Wherever he turned, the echoes were there, and little images that he had dampened down for twenty years bombarded him from all sides. Robert, Robert, Robert, and all the pictures happy ones.

'I'm here, Pa, I'm here. I'll never leave you, Daddy. Find me, find me.'

The tears were streaming down his cheeks and he threw up his face to the sun that was trying to reach him through the trees, his trees, trees that would have been Robert's and would be Jamie's.

'I've found you, my darling boy,' he said, as for the first time in over twenty years he walked into his ancestral home, 'and I'll never leave you.'

Episode 7

Las Estrellitas, Mexico, 1940

The party to mark the betrothal of his daughter, Carlota, had been a resounding success. They were, as his wife murmured nauseatingly, *in love.*

'Love,' a lesser man than Don Jose Luis Alcantarilla-Medina might have been said to have snorted as his thin aristocratic lips formed the word. 'What good has being in love ever done this family?'

Carlota to be married and soon Teresa, and Lucia would follow their older sister. Don Jose Luis looked forward to the advent of grandchildren, grandsons he said loudly in case God was not listening carefully, grandsons.

Lucia. The beloved name came into his mind and he sat down heavily at the ornate desk. Lucia, his baby sister, who had been forced to marry that gringo, and who had died in child bed.

But her child was a boy. The knowledge smote Don Jose Luis like the blow of a hammer. Lucia had had a son, who was, the words stuck in his proud throat, a legitimate heir to these acres, and Alvaro had hidden him, fearing his wrath. Great heavens he was not an illiterate bandido, he was Don Jose Luis Alcantarilla-Medina and father of three ... daughters. It was never too late to make amends. For La Dama Lucia he would find her son and show him the unimaginable wealth and power that could be his. He should marry Lucia, his cousin, who was, after all, a very lovely young woman.

Unaware that his life was being so ruthlessly planned for him Alejandro Alcantarilla-Medina was sitting at the piano in the drawing room of his friend Jamie's Edinburgh home.

'Clementi,' he told Jamie who was singularly unimpressed by his playing, 'a sadly under rated composer.'

If the Honorable James Fotheringham was unimpressed by his talent most of the music schools of Europe were not. Several of the most prestigious had offered to train the young pianist but – the world had changed overnight. Europe was at war but Mexico, the land of his birth, was not.

Xandro crashed his hands down on the keys in a very discordant sound and Jamie looked up and laughed lightly. 'Don't break it, take the whole thing.'

'I'm sorry, Jamie, and I hope Lord Inchmarnock didn't hear that but, dear God, Jamie, what am I going to do? I don't belong here, Senor Himenez says I'm not welcome in Mexico, and now because of this damned Hitler I can't study in Vienna.'

'You'll do well in Glasgow.'

'But I should fight. I can't sit through the war playing the piano.'

Jamie made himself more comfortable on the sofa. 'Don't see why not. What did Mum say?'

Lady Inchmarnock had vetoed the idea with her usual practicality. 'But you are Mexican, Xandro, and there are more than enough boys rushing into uniform. The Arts are the nucleus of human expression, my dear, they civilise us. That is your mission, to remind us all that we are meant for greater things that killing one another. Stay in Scotland to study. We will be able to see you and be your family, that is, if you would like us to be.'

Family. What a beautiful word.

'You have all these people to love you, Alejandro,' he told himself 'You have enough money and you have some talent. Stop feeling sorry for yourself and work.'

Because he loved and respected Lady Inchmarnock he had enrolled at the Royal Scottish Academy of Music and Drama in Glasgow where he would study piano and conducting.

'I wish I was good at something, Xandro,' said Jamie from the sofa. 'I've known you for ever and all you have ever wanted to do was play your old piano. I was raised knowing that I inherit an ancient title, immense privilege, and responsibility. What have I ever wanted to do? Farm in Australia, I suppose.'

'Can't you do that?'

Jamie threw a cushion at his head. 'No, stoopid. 1. Pa has hired a good manager. 2.

There's a war on.' He was silent for a moment and then his irrepressible humour broke through. 'Wouldn't it be fun if we could join up together and take on the baddies the way we used to do at school?'

'I really don't think we'd get very far sneaking into Germany and soaking Hitler's sheets,' said Alejandro dryly.

'Don't see why not.' Jamie jumped to his feet and put a forefinger across his upper lip. Then in a very poor imitation of a German accent he said, 'Ze war is over because we have all the very bad colds and need to go to the San.'

Xandro laughed as Jamie collapsed in a large heap on his sofa again. 'You'll enjoy university, Jamie, and it will adore you. And much more important, Lady Flora has said you are my family so we can see each other at the breaks, and I will keep you in your place.'

Jamie smiled. 'That's good but, gosh Xandro, it can't be the same for you because you're not British but I want to do my bit. All our friends from school are joining up and because of Dad I have to be a good boy and go to the university and spend the war playing rugby.'

'It is the same for me, Jamie. I would like

to *do my bit* but Lady Flora says I must learn to play the piano so that I can help civilise the world after the war. We will need the Arts but we will also need doctors and lawyers and teachers and plumbers and, and, and.'

'And not one of them could I possibly do.'

'I think you could be any one of them. Your problem is that God has been too good to you, *Dishonourable* James Fotheringham. You should have had a few years of Mother Mercedes.'

'I did. We called it Prep. School. Let's go downstairs and keep Dad company. Mummy was supposed to come home but no sign of her yet.'

'That is something you could do, Jamie, help your mother at the hospital.'

Shocked, Jamie stopped in mid flight on the stairs. 'Moi, in a hospital? What could I possibly do?'

'Moral support for all the pretty nurses. You will see, I will come also to do my bit.'

'Pretty nurses? In the army? You have been day dreaming, amigo mio.'

'This is not a good idea.' Constance Faraday stopped at the top of the staircase and peered over the huge pile of mail in her arms. Really she ought to do it in two trips but she so wanted to impress the formidable Lady Inchmarnock who, she was quite sure, thought that she was impossibly ill equipped to be her secretary.

'But she's got to keep me, she just has to and I'll learn quickly. I always do,' said Constance bravely and set off down the stairs.

Perhaps if they had decided to leave the carpet the descent would have been easier but Lady Inchmarnock had decided to have the splendid old carpets replaced by hard wearing utilitarian carpets. Scores of young men would hobble up and down those stairs in the next few years. The carpets had not yet been laid and the polished wood shone.

So tense that she was hardly breathing Constance was almost at the foot. She would have the study arranged as neatly as possible and Lady Inchmarnock would be so surprised by the swift change that she would let her stay.

And then her heel caught, possibly on a nail. Constance threw out her arms to save herself and the letters and packages went flying down the stairs to reach the foot of the stairs just as the owner and, more importantly, the Director of the Inchmarnock hospital opened the front door. The mail was followed swiftly by Constance who regained her balance but not her poise.

Lady Inchmarnock steadied her, looked down at her shoes, said 'You'll break your neck in those ridiculous things, change them at once,' and then went into her study and closed the door gently but firmly behind her.

'Blast, blast, blast,' silently screamed poor Constance and she kicked the nearest pile of offending post farther across the expanse of hall.

Meanwhile Lady Inchmarnock sat down at her husband's desk in his former study and surveyed, with some dismay, the enormous pile of correspondence.

'Where can I begin?' she asked herself, 'and especially if that empty-headed young socialite is the best they can do for a secretary for me.'

Luckily for Constance, Lady Inchmarnock remembered that many, many years ago before she had entered Medical School, the opinion of most adults was that she too was empty-headed.

'I've made it as neat as possible, Ma'am,' said Constance as she slipped into the room later, 'but I'm afraid there's even more and that doesn't begin to take into account the lists.'

'Lists?' asked Flora faintly.

'Supplies, to the last safety pin – we need lists.'

'With copies, I suppose.'

''Fraid so, Ma'am.'

Lady Inchmarnock took a deep breath and folded her hands neatly on top of the pile. 'Then if we are ever to get anything useful done in this hospital, like taking care of the wounded for instance, we had better make the dratted lists.'

'You could put: No 1. Patients.'

Oh, her dratted tongue. Constance looked anxiously at her employer. Should Lady Inchmarnock think her impertinent as well as inefficient she might dispense with her services and Constance desperately wanted to – what was it her brothers said – do her bit.

Flora looked up at the girl. 'Well, well, well, I hoped there was some humour inside those ridiculous shoes. Yes, No 1. Patients, and I'm afraid Constance, just in case my husband should ever come in to this room, you'll have to find me another desk.'

'Yes, Lady Inchmarnock.'

If she was curious she was too well bred to

159

ask. Yes, indeed, thought Flora, if she can type we should get along very well.

'What's your speed, Constance?'

The Honorable Constance Faraday blushed rosily. 'Typing, you mean. I'm awfully sorry but I'm just learning. I'll do things over and over – in my own time, Ma'am,' she added hurriedly, 'and I'll get them right. Please, I do so want to help and I learn quickly. Really I do.'

'You won't have any *own time*,' said Flora dryly. She looked down at the desk 'Let's make a start anyway.'

They spent the rest of the morning on the inventories. Flora was determined to make this idea work. Inchmarnock House would spend the duration of the war as a hospital but when she had conceived of the idea she had had no real notion of just what a mammoth task she had taken on. Some of the huge stately rooms on the ground floor had been converted easily into dormitories but the kitchens and bathrooms had required extensive modernisation and then a lift had had to be installed.

Sandy's study she was keeping as the administrative offices. It had a beautiful French door leading out on to the terrace and glimpses of the gardens would certainly

160

rest her mind when she was over worked. All the old family pictures had been taken down and Flora had hung several charming water colours on the walls and, while there were flowers still grown in the gardens, she was determined to have at least one bowl of flowers somewhere in the room. Soon the flower gardens would be changed over to vegetable production, sensible but a little sad too. At least there would still be flowers in the woods around the house.

The girl had worked hard. She was completely untrained but then, *so were you when you first went to Medical School,* Lady Inchmarnock reminded herself, and the girl was willing. She would give her a chance.

'I'm going home at weekends until we are up and running, Constance. If you have nothing better to do, you're welcome.' She saw the dubious expression that flitted for a second across her secretary's face. 'I have a son. He's younger than you, of course, but if there is any young life in Edinburgh he will have found it.'

'Thank you, Lady Inchmarnock. For now I need to spend as much time as possible mastering that typewriter but perhaps one weekend, if it's not an imposition. My own home is in Surrey. Too far, of course, and

161

then there'll be rationing and train travel will be difficult, I imagine.'

'So you're like me, Constance, you feel we're in for a long haul.'

'Women should run the world, Lady Inchmarnock.'

'A feminist?'

'A realist.'

They laughed amicably.

'Well, off you go and try to make neat copies of those lists.'

She was going to give her a chance. Constance was thrilled. She would prove how capable she was, she would. She pushed her chair back, picked up the pile of lists and then, at the same time, attempted to pick up the portable typewriter which was all the War Office had been able to find for them at this point. It hit the vase of flowers on the director's desk.

Lady Inchmarnock closed her eyes for a moment while her secretary dabbed ineffectually at the spilled water with a wisp of lace handkerchief

'Go away, Constance. And on Monday, sensible shoes and sensible handkerchiefs.'

Constance fled.

Nellie Sinclair was a realist. She had worked

hard all her life doing her best for her husband and family and she had prayed to see her only son become a doctor. She had day dreamed a little of walking past his smart office with the shining brass plate that said Doctor James Bains Sinclair but that, it seemed, was like all day dreams, ready to disappear.

If there had been hard work and dismay during the past twenty years she could not remember. Her memories were only of Tam, Jimmy and Flora, and all full of sunshine and laughter. Were they ever cold, dirty, hungry? No, she remembered only warmth and love.

And here was she rationed to four ounces of butter and twelve ounces of sugar. What was this idiot government thinking on? A good cook used that and mair in a day. Bacon, four ounces if it was uncooked and three and a half ounces if she bought it cooked. Me, Nellie Bains, buying cooked ham frae a butcher! That'll be the day! And meat rationing coming.

Nellie surveyed her full store cupboard with its large bowl of preserved eggs and then slammed the door closed. It was not the government and its rationing that was making her angry. It was Jimmy being away

163

with this Army Medical Corps.

She was still indulging in a good cry when Tam found her.

'It was the eggs,' she tried to explain. 'They sat there looking at me, reminding me of Jimmy and how he never ever did owt wrong.'

Tam remembered many occasions when Jimmy's naughtiness had resulted in a good wallop from one or other of his parents but he said nothing now in betrayal of the paragon.

'Aye, he was a good boy and he'll be a good doctor too. Just you wait till you see him in his uniform, Nellie. Officers get wee pips on their shooders.'

'Does their fancy wee pips stop bullets?'

What could he answer to that?

'It's 1940, Tam, no the Middle Ages,' Nellie, refusing comfort, went on. 'This war'll last a year maybe at the outside; he should stay at hame where it's nice and safe and take care of the ill folk here. You went tae the trenches tae keep him here in safety.'

Again Tam had no answer but just then there was a tremendous rapping at the heavy oak door and a dishevelled Flora Welborn almost fell in when Tam opened it.

'Nellie, Nellie, come quick, Nancy's hurt.'

Eddie Welborn was sitting at his office window just looking out. He saw nothing. That is, he saw his wife, Victoria, and he saw their years of, what he had thought, happy marriage spread out there on the gravel. He had been happy, ecstatically so. He had a lovely wife, two beautiful, loving, funny daughters and a farm that took all his energy. What else did a person need?

Obviously Victoria needed something more and she was out there somewhere looking for it. He had known she was bright: that was one of the things that had attracted him but, at her age, to be going to lectures at the university and talking about taking classes. No wonder he had snapped impatiently at Nancy. He was always snapping, that was what Flora had said when she had gone racing after her sister.

'You and Mum just bicker bicker bicker. Well, I'm fed up, Daddy and so is Nancy. One of these days we'll go and live with Granny and then where will you be?'

Where indeed? But he and Victoria did not bicker. They were much too civilised. In fact they hardly ever talked these days.

He heard a horse and a shout and looked up.

Outside the window his stable boy was trying to talk Nancy out of riding the huge stallion that she had saddled.

'He's too strong for ye, Nancy. Get aff right now or I'll shout for yer dad.'

Eddie jumped to his feet and banged the window with his fist. Nancy, startled, turned to look at him and Eddie saw terror chase the surprise off her young face as Ajax, aware that she had lost control of his reins, reared up and then bucked throwing his too light young burden over his head onto the ground. Her father stood paralysed. He could not move, he could not scream and then as the great horse, content to have won the one sided fight skittered happily over to the water trough, Eddie found control of his limbs.

He ran, the blood turning to ice in his veins, his heart squeezed by an ice cold hand. Nancy lay quiet in a curiously defenceless heap, her right arm twisted horribly beneath her. Eddie fell to his knees beside her and then Eddie heard Flora scream.

She came running from the stables to throw herself down on top of her sister.

That settled Eddie. He pulled her off. 'Flora, Flora, calm down right now. Go and phone Mum. She's at Granny Menmuir's. He prayed inside that she was. 'Flora, I need your help,' he said again, almost shaking the sobbing girl. 'If you can't get Mummy, go and get Nellie. And for God's sake, Jack, phone for an ambulance.'

The dazzling notes of the music went spiralling through the air and floated off into the afternoon air. For a time the composer was content to have the piano alone assault the senses and then he brought in the huge comforting blanket of the orchestra to echo the triumphant notes.

'Unbelievable,' breathed Victoria as she released her tightly held breath.

Emil smiled. 'Not unbelievable, Victoria, Beethoven. Concerto number one. I'm glad that the Rondo is just less than nine minutes long; I doubt you could hold your breath any longer.'

She blushed delightfully. 'Was I holding my breath? It was just so wonderful.'

They were sitting in the living room of Elsie's little flat in Dundee. It had become so easy to pop in once a week to water the plants and then one day it had rained heavily and, forced to wait for a while, Emil had said that what was missing was music.

Now each week it was an event and was rapidly becoming the most important hour or so of Victoria's week. Each time they met he brought one of his records. Elsie's ancient Vitrola was brought out of the cupboard under the stairs and Victoria discovered a world that she had scarcely believed existed. Emil was cultured and educated. He could speak easily and knowledgeably about art and music and books, and not only Polish ones but British and French, German and Italian, and even, who would have thought it, American.

Victoria responded to his teachings as a flower, deprived of rain, responds to a spring shower. What if she had never met him? She had been perfectly happy never having heard a Mozart symphony or a Beethoven concerto, had she not. But how much richer life was now, just because of her friendship with this dear man.

She said *friendship* defiantly. Well she knew how the tongues would wag but there was nothing wrong in extending the hand of friendship to a refugee. That was all she was doing, was she not. At the beginning of their friendship she had suggested that he visit her home and she should ask him to a Sunday meal with them, and she would, she would. Right now she was enjoying just getting to know someone from such a different world.

'Shall we play the other side, Victoria? It is a Bagatelle and quite charming.'

Victoria smiled her agreement. She loved his taste in Classical music. When she was listening every sense in her body was alert, quivering, relishing the moment.

'I am enjoying your music, Emil,' she said.

He smiled at her as he put the record on again and then, instead of returning to his own seat, he sat down on the sofa beside Victoria. She was conscious of his size, of the faint clean smell of him. She tingled and wished, oh what did she wish?

'It is everybody's music, my dear,' said Emil who seemed blissfully unaware of the effect that he or, indeed, the music was having. 'Beethoven wrote for the masses. You British are so ready to label everything for this class or that class. Music is just music. Now sit back and listen.'

She did but it was difficult to concentrate on the music with him so close. She could feel the warmth of his arm through her thin blouse and for some reason she shivered.

The music drew to its exquisite close. 'You see, Victoria, a Bagatelle, a little thing, negli-

169

gible, a trifle. That is how he saw it.'

'It was a delightful trifle.'

He was looking at her and the air seemed heavy, charged with electricity, as it is just before a thunder storm. She had to break the spell.

She smiled. 'Tell me about your daughter. Does she like Beethoven?'

It was the wrong thing to say. His face that had been relaxed and almost young became drawn and the eyes bleak. 'Yes, a nice Polish girl who admires a German composer. She likes also Richard Wagner but I cannot bring myself to introduce him to you, Victoria. I am not so broad minded as my little girl.

'I don't understand,' Victoria began.

'Wagner does not like Jews. Anneliese forgives him for his narrow mind because he is, she says, a genius. I am not a genius and therefore my daughter says I am *stuffy* because I refuse to listen.'

Victoria looked up, hope in her eyes. '*She says*. You have heard from her?'

He got up and took the record from the turn table and then he made a great business of carefully putting it inside first its paper and then its cardboard sleeve. He shook his head, almost as if he was tired and wished to shake the sleepiness away. 'We should go now, I think.'

Unaware of everything except the need to give him comfort Victoria went to him and put her arms around him and he buried his face on her shoulder. She held him for a moment and then, almost tentatively he put his arms around her, and they stood quietly, saying nothing.

At last Victoria took control. 'Come and sit down, dear friend.' Why did she call him friend?

'Emil, don't bottle your terrors up inside.'

He sighed and released her. 'You are right, Victoria. How practical women are.'

They moved back into the small sitting room and Victoria sat down and held out her arms to him. He stood for a moment and then he gasped and sat down quickly beside her on the over stuffed sofa.

'If I say the name of my terror I make it exist, Victoria. Can you understand?'

He put his arms around her and held her as if she was a life belt and he was in grave danger of drowning.

There was such naked fear in his voice that Victoria gasped. 'My grandfather was the most important person in my life while I was a little girl, Emil. He always said, a trouble shared is a trouble halved. I don't want to intrude but...'

Suddenly he hugged her to him with such strength and longing that Victoria could do nothing but submit and yet, as quickly as he had held her, he let her go. 'Forgive me, such kindness. My wife used to say the same. One lovely Polish girl, one lovely Scot, and they say the same thing when there is trouble. No, Victoria, I have not heard. I ring the Embassy every day. I have tried to contact friends but there is no news. Maybe my daughter is living quite happily, going every day to the university and trusting me to work and pray here until we can be together. She has her friends and her Ivan but there is a monster loose in Europe, Victoria, and no-one is safe from his madness, especially not a little Jewish girl whose doting papa listened to her pleading and did not demand that she accompany him to Scotland. I knew what was happening. Dear God, Victoria, how many of us have closed our eyes. Sometimes I think I should start to walk to Poland, walk like the little children in the Crusades, and find my daughter.'

'They all died, Emil, the Children's Crusade. You can do more here.'

He pushed her away and stood up. 'I can

172

do nothing, nothing. You can't imagine what I feel, so useless, so helpless, and so at fault. Sometimes I think I will go crazy. Every night I am on my knees and no answers, no answers. Come we are here too long and I am afraid that perhaps I can no longer control myself.'

She looked up at him and for a second exulted in the look in his eyes and then she remembered that she was a married woman and she feared it.

Wordlessly she put the gramophone away in its dark home under the stairs and then made sure the gas fire was off. She took out her purse and fed the ravenous gas meter with the few shillings lurking at the bottom.

'I never have a shilling when I need one,' she said but Emil was not listening.

Guiltily she realised that she had forgotten to water the plants but that was a small sacrifice to pay and she could easily come back into town later in the week.

She fixed a smile to her face and walked into the hall for her coat. 'On Sunday you must come and have a good Scottish Sunday dinner with us, Emil,' she said in an appalling attempt at being natural.

The day that had been so perfect was now so overshadowed with a black grasping shadow that stretched all the way from Poland.

'I am not good company,' he began but she refused to listen.

'My Nancy and her chatter, chatter will help, and maybe by Sunday you'll have had a letter. We must never give up hope.'

He looked at her bleakly and she flushed with embarrassment. Nancy was not the only one of the family who took refuge in idle chatter.

'I'm sorry, Emil. Of course I can't begin to know how you feel. But I am a mother and I am your friend. Let me help.'

He looked into her eyes and, for a moment, his beautiful eyes were warm, and – no, she must not think them loving. The light of friendship, perhaps.

'You have helped, Victoria, and I would like to meet your family and this little Nancy who will chatter all during dinner about her horses. And I too, will be a bore and impress her with my knowledge of the great Polish cavalry regiments.'

She reached past him for her coat and perhaps he misinterpreted her action for the next minute she was in his arms and he was holding her as if she was very precious and liable to break.

'Oh, Victoria,' he groaned. 'I have waited for so many years to find you.'

At first she did not understand. 'To find me...' she began and she looked into his eyes and could not doubt what she saw there.

And then he bent down, closer and closer, and his lips met hers.

Her mind worked furiously. 'I am mad, mad, and I should push him away,' but she did not and gently, tentatively, her arms stole up and round his neck and she returned the kiss which was no longer gentle.

Episode 8

Victoria Welborn and her husband sat on opposite sides of the waiting room at the Royal Infirmary and looked, not at one another, but at the floor. If there was comfort to be found there, its effects were not readily apparent.

'My baby,' Victoria sobbed, but only inside her heart and mind. Her face showed nothing but shock and fear. 'If I had been there she would never have been so disobedient. She always knows, both of them

175

do, just how to make Eddie do exactly what they want.'

Victoria could not bring herself to face the fact that when her younger daughter had been thrown from the stallion she had been ... she had been with another man.

'If anything happens ... if she dies...' Victoria's hands clenched and unclenched themselves and Eddie watched and wanted to hold his wife, to give and take comfort, but he did not know this quiet woman. He could not reach her.

The door opened to admit Catriona Menmuir and immediately the atmosphere changed. A breath of fresh Angus air swept much of the misery from the unattractive sterile little room.

'Is there any news?' asked Catriona after she had hugged, first her daughter and then her son-in-law.

Victoria shook her head. She could not find the mechanism that would make her voice work.

'Operations take a long time,' said Eddie helping Catriona, who was least in need of assistance at this time, to a chair.

'She's a strong, healthy lassie,' said Catriona with an attempt at a smile. 'You'll see. She'll be up and about in no time.' She

176

looked from one to the other. 'Eddie, love, I could kill for a cup of tea. Would you see what you can find?'

When he went off immediately as she had known he would, Catriona went over and sat down beside Victoria. She took her daughter's cold hands in hers.

'Victoria, what's happened to you? My daughter would have been comforting her man through his fear and worry as she always comforted her mother and her grandfather before that. What's happened to you and Eddie that at a time like this you sit like strangers.'

Victoria raised her despairing eyes to her mother's. 'You don't understand: you can't.'

'Try me, lass. There's some grief eating away at you, or is it some guilt?' she added astutely.

Victoria started in her chair and tried to withdraw her hands but Catriona's hands, old work worn hands, were too strong. 'Victoria, there's a wee lassie fighting, maybe for her life. Nothing else comes near that.'

The sweet relief of tears. 'I can't presume to comfort him, Mum. I'm so ashamed.' She was quiet for a moment and then it spilled out. 'Nothing happened, not really, there was nothing wrong, but, oh, Mum, they couldn't find me to tell me about Nancy.'

'They couldn't find me either. I was having tea at Draffens.'

'I was having tea too, with a ... friend, a professor.'

Catriona was quiet, remembering perhaps her first husband, Victoria's father who had 'had tea' with too many friends. She said a silent prayer for guidance. 'You're here now, Victoria, and Eddie needs his wife and Nancy and Flora need their mother.'

Eddie and a nurse entered together. The nurse was smiling. 'You can see her now, just for a minute, but it's unlikely she'll recognise you. That's the sedation. Just Mum and Dad,' she added as Catriona stood up, 'and Mrs Welborn, please don't be upset by all the bandages and tubes.'

Instinctively Victoria reached for Eddie's hand as they approached the bed where their younger daughter was lying. Eddie had served in the trenches of the war and Victoria's friend, the Honorable Robert Fotheringham had been horrifically wounded there. The Welborns had seen injury and its aftermath before. But this small frail bandaged body was their daughter, their baby. They clung to one another, their eyes still fixed on the small inert form on the clinical white bed.

'Her spine is fine,' said the nurse. She looked Victoria straight in the eyes. 'It will be a whilie before we can tell about other damage. She was thrown on her head, you see. I'm sorry, but it's best you should be prepared.'

The Honorable James Fotheringham completed his first term at the University of Edinburgh. To his own surprise, and possibly to his father's, he did very well in the examinations.

'A fluke,' said Jamie.

'I wouldn't call you a natural academic, old man, but you've done well,' said his father as he wrestled with the huge Christmas tree that had arrived that afternoon from Inchmarnock House. He looked across at his son who was, as usual, draped over a settee. 'Come on, Jamie, I want this blasted thing decorated before your mother gets here.'

Jamie laughed as he uncoiled himself. 'Proper sacred Christmas spirit, Dad. *Blasted thing* is not how one should refer to a Christmas tree.'

'Do you want it decorated or don't you?'

'Leave it for old Xandro. Mexicans love all the tinselly bits of Christmas. Dad, I have to talk to you.'

'I know, that's why it's better if we work on the tree.'

'Then you probably know what I want to say too.'

'Yes, and the answer is no. You may not join the Army.'

'That wasn't my question. Dad, they'll conscript me; it's not going to be over for a very longtime. Better that I join what I want to join, than be sent willy-nilly...'

The discussion, if discussion it was, was interrupted by the entrance of Jamie's friend, Alejandro Alcantarilla-Medina, followed a few minutes later by Jamie's mother and, to the evident delight of both young men, a very pretty girl.

'This is Constance Faraday, my secretary. Connie is spending a few days with us until we can get her a ticket to London.'

Connie stepped forward to shake hands with her host and stepped on a box of Christmas baubles. Lord and Lady Inchmarnock looked at one another and smiled. Flora had told Sandy often enough of her new secretary's inadequacies.

It was Jamie who diffused the situation.

He fell to his knees and began picking up the bits. 'Connie, you angel,' he said. 'I have hated these silly things for years and Mummy insists on dragging them out Christmas after Christmas.

Xandro and Connie joined him on the carpet and if Connie wondered that such old family ornaments still had a brand new price tag on them, she smiled, and fell, who knows, a little in love with Jamie.

After dinner, she fell a little in love with Xandro who played Mozart and Chopin for them and then the latest hits, 'When you wish upon a star,' 'The last time I saw Paris' and even 'South of the Border,' before playing especially for Flora, Christmas carols.

'You are fantastic, Xandro,' said Connie.

'Get his autograph now,' said Jamie, 'while he's still poor and unknown. This is the Royal Scottish Academy's best piano student and Mexico's loss, Scotland's gain.' He looked straight at his father who flinched a little, as if preparing to ward off the blow that was coming. 'Maybe old Xandro will play in the Officers' Mess for me, Dad. I've been accepted by the Air Force.'

There was a frightening silence. Lady Inchmarnock looked at her husband who was swaying a little as he held on to the back of the seat in front of him.

'The Air Force, Darling,' she tried to smile. 'Better than being conscripted, I suppose, but the family has always been army, you know.'

He smiled at her gratefully and turned to his father. 'Daddy, please understand. It was coming, you know, and I'm fascinated by planes. Please.'

'I have a brother in the Air Force,' said Connie into the unnerving silence. 'He swears planes are the safest place to be, Jamie, except your feet get so damned cold.'

Still Jamie looked despairingly at his father and still Lord Inchmarnock stood holding the back of the chair. He was remembering a beautiful schoolboy who had lied about his age and gone, tragically, to war. At last he let go of the chair.

'I didn't realise how much like your brother you are, you brat, but I'll be dashed if I'll congratulate you. I'm sure your mother will find you warm socks.'

'Just accept, Dad, please.'

'Accept?' Lord Inchmarnock looked at his wife. 'How much are we supposed to accept, old girl?'

'Everything that's thrown at us, my dear, like all the other parents, all over Europe.'

'Wait,' said Xandro suddenly into the tension. He closed the piano and stood up. 'Lord Sandy, I have a letter I want you to see. The strangest thing. Would you believe that I am not Mexican at all, but Scottish, and you, Lady Flora, know my family.'

He ran up to his room, the room where he had spent so many happy holidays, a lonely confused little boy, growing up in a country so far from what he had always known as home. When he returned it was obvious from all the expressions of interest that Lady Inchmarnock had brought her secretary up to date with what she knew of his history. He handed Lord Inchmarnock a fat letter and then smiled and took it back. It was in Spanish.

'This is from Don Jose-Luis Alcantarilla-Medina who is, he says, my uncle, the brother of my mother Lucia and of my uncle Alvaro. I don't know why he has suddenly decided to tell me everything but it seems I am not wholly Mexican. See, this is a marriage certificate.'

They all looked and could understand nothing – except one name.

John Cameron.

Flora and Sandy looked at each other. They knew that name. Of course they did.

John Cameron was Catriona Menmuir's first husband and Victoria Welborn's father.

They looked now at Xandro who was laughing in genuine amusement. 'It seems this John Cameron married Lucia Alcantarilla-Medina and I am their son. I am also, according to my uncle, the rightful heir to property owned by my father, this John Cameron, in Scotland. John Cameron told the Alcantarillas that he owned vast acres. I am not a Mexican peasant, Jamie, as you always told people, but a Scottish landlord.'

Several old memories followed one another through Lady Flora's mind. 'I am happy that you have discovered your family, Xandro...' she began, 'but this will come as a great shock...'

'To the nice lady I played to at that funeral? Tell me, Lady Flora, is she my grandmother and will she want to know me? Today it seems that everyone wants me. This uncle says I own property in Mexico. Me, Xandro who lived in an orphanage with a nun for a mother and no family. Now I find I have two.'

'And us,' smiled Jamie slapping him on the back and looking again at his pale, stunned father. 'That makes three. Right, Dad?'

Xandro managed to smile. 'The Camerons, Lady Flora, can you tell me about them?'

Lord Inchmarnock smiled in forgiveness at his only son and moved over to put a log on the fire. He looked at his wife and she sat back quietly in her chair. 'Xandro, why do you think you're the Cameron heir, not that there's a great deal to inherit. No vast acres, lad, a small farm, no more?'

'I am the legitimate male heir, Lord Sandy. Unless I have an elder brother, then, of course, he is the heir of our father.'

'No, Xandro, there's no legitimate elder brother. A sister, and, Flora, this is going to come as a shock, but if John Cameron did not will that farm to Victoria, then according to Scots law, it belongs to his legitimate son.'

'Me,' said Xandro. 'I think, perhaps, my sister will not wish to know me.'

New Year's Day, 1941 found the capital city of Edinburgh a picture postcard wonderland of white. Professor Emil Piaseczany did not see the beauty. He did not hear the happy laughter of the young serviceman hanging out of the windows of the august Overseas League as they tried to catch and return the snowballs thrown by other servicemen on the street. He could only hear the voice of his old friend.

She was taken, Emil, with every other Jew in the street. We're not sure when: sometime before Christmas. They've been taken to camps but where we can't say. Germany, maybe or even in Poland. They're work camps, Emil, not death camps. You have to believe that...

He thought he could no longer believe anything. His little Anneliese, his child, in a camp somewhere and he could not even find her. He was here, safe in this beautiful country. He had more than enough to eat, he had money in his pocket and a comfortable flat in which to live. Civilised conversation surrounded him and music when he needed its solace. But he could no longer even believe in music.

Schonberg, Stravinsky, Bartok, Hindemith, were among the wave of great musicians who had left Europe and gone to live in the United States. America was not at war. Perhaps they believed they could compose great music in a peaceful land. Who would be left in Europe to hear it when this madness was over? His daughter had disappeared. While he dazzled students with his reputation and, he hoped, the sense in his lectures, his innocent trusting little girl had been bundled into a cattle truck and taken God knows where. And why? Why? Because she was Jewish. How could this insane world claim that it was civilised?

'Happy New Year, old man,' yelled one of the boy soldiers.

Old man. Yesterday I was fifty two years old. Today I am an old man. He stared at the boy and saw that he was not much older than Anneliese. The boy was playing in the snow, playing, like a child, with snowballs.

'I must not hate for if I hate this boy because he plays in the snow then I am no better than the thug who threw my Anneliese in that truck. I must not hate.'

Emil bent quickly and formed a ball from the soft white snow and there were tears of incalculable pain running down his cheeks as he threw it at the young soldier.

'Happy New Year yourself,' he tried to shout, but the words would not come out because the boy was a boy and the boy was a soldier and today he played in the snow and tomorrow, oh, dear God in Heaven, where would the boy soldier be?

Stumbling like the old man he resembled Emil headed for Waverley Station. He had to get back to Dundee. He had to see Victoria.

Victoria was clean and fresh and sane and she would tell him that Anneliese was well and he would let the music of her soft Scottish voice wash over him and he would not hate.

He had never telephoned her at the farm. In fact he had never telephoned her. They met, always as if by chance, at the university. Then sometimes Victoria would say, 'I'm going to Elsie's flat to water the plants. Would you like a cup of tea?'

He had telephoned from Perth while he waited for a connection to Dundee. What a journey it had been. The train had been late and, as always, these days, was packed full of men and women in uniform. He had had to stand most of the way. These soldiers did not laugh and shout. Their eyes were too red rimmed from lack of sleep and still too full of sights they had seen. They had moved like automatons at each station as the carriages had emptied and filled up again. Now many of them stood swaying with exhaustion on the platform while they too waited for connecting trains.

'Victoria? Hello, it's Emil.'

She said nothing for a moment and he thought perhaps he had made a mistake.

'Victoria?' he asked again.

'Hello, Emil. Happy New Year, it's nice of you to ring.'

'I had to talk to you. Can we meet, just to talk, for a cup of tea?' Desperately he fed more coppers into the telephone. 'Victoria?'

'I'm sorry, Emil, I won't be back at the lectures.'

'Elsie's plants.'

'Plants? I forgot all about them.' He could not doubt that she told the truth.

'Emil, I have to go. I'm visiting my little girl in the hospital in a few minutes. Goodbye.'

He said, 'Goodbye,' to an empty line and stood there listening to silence. Then he carefully replaced the receiver.

The hospital? Her little girl? He had to get to Dundee.

'Mister, you'll miss your train if you stand there keeping that phone warm all day.'

He ran and did not notice that he stood all the way to Dundee too. It began to snow as he walked up Reform Street and by the time he reached the Infirmary he was colder and hungrier and more tired than he could ever remember having been and he welcomed the sensations because he shared them with Anneliese.

'I am looking for a Miss Welborn,' he told

189

the receptionist. 'Flora or maybe, it is Nancy.'

'There's a Nancy Welborn in Intensive Care.' She directed him through the warren that was Dundee's splendid hospital to the ward where Nancy Welborn lay silent in her bed. Victoria was sitting holding the girl's hand.

From his own grief he spoke to her. 'Victoria, I do not wish to intrude...' He stopped as she looked up at him and saw the brief light of welcome in her eyes.

She lowered her head. 'Emil,' she said quietly. 'I have been too busy to ring you.'

'I'm sorry, my dear friend. I did not know. May I stay for a few minutes with you? Can you tell me what has happened?'

She knew he meant to her daughter and not to their friendship. 'She was thrown from a horse. Her bones are healing but she hasn't regained consciousness.'

Somewhere in the depths of her own misery she remembered that he too worried over the fate of a child but her grief was so strong, her guilt too overwhelming.

She felt his hand, for a second, like the touch of a butterfly on her shoulder. And in spite of herself she remembered a kiss that was almost as gentle, a kiss to which she had given herself, willingly, despairingly.

'I will pray for her,' he said and she heard the sound of his tired footsteps on the way back along the ugly linoleum covered floor. Did she also hear, 'as I pray for my own'? She did not know but she knew that the cold place that was her heart was a little warmer. Later she would wonder why he looked so exhausted and even unshaven but, for now, she was content merely to cherish that one moment of human contact.

She held her daughter's hand. 'I'll bring some records, Nancy. Beethoven, such lovely music and you'll hear it and come back to me.'

In March Andrew Menmuir, Catriona's son was arrested in Glasgow. The charge was trading on the Black Market.

He had been arrested in a joint operation conducted by the Glasgow city police department and the military police. The civil police had informed the military police that one Andrew Menmuir, private, first class, was involved in stealing and reselling alcohol, petrol, tyres, and the one that Catriona found unforgivable, foodstuffs. How could a boy who had wanted for nothing steal from those who had nothing?

Like too many mothers she wondered again what she had done wrong. Why was her son going to jail and being thrown out of the Army, in disgrace? Even in a war, Britain did not need the services of Andrew Menmuir. The grief, and yes, the humiliation, was overwhelming. Was there anyone with whom she could share her unhappiness? Impossible to add one more burden to Victoria's grief. Nancy seemed still to be in a complete coma although Victoria argued with the doctors.

'She's responding to the music. I'm sure she is. I know her fingers tried to move. I felt it.'

Catriona encouraged her daughter to believe and she did not tell her of her brother's disgrace.

One morning, early in April, she was surprised and delighted to have a telephone call from her old friend and former lodger, Flora Fotheringham. Oh, the relief. Here was someone who would listen and not judge and hold her hand as she cried as she had held all those years ago

'The house is up and running as a hospital, Catriona, and I do want Victoria to come and see it, take away her memory of it but I know she has her hands full now.

Later, in the summer perhaps. But you, old friend. Can't you drive over and have lunch with me.'

So Catriona found herself being driven through the gates that lead to Inchmarnock House. It was too early for rhododendrons but she could see clumps of primroses nestling almost at the feet of stately daffodil bulbs. There were crocuses too, yellow and white, purple and orange and trees, such magnificent trees. The car swept round a wide driveway – 'They called this a carriage sweep in the Olden Days, Mrs Menmuir. A lot grander than driveway, is it no?' said her driver – and there was the beautiful old house, sitting in what had once been formal rose gardens but which now, to Catriona's expert eyes, showed rows and rows of germinating vegetables.

A very pretty young girl in a rather unattractive uniform opened the door. 'Do come in, Mrs Menmuir. I'm Connie Faraday, Lady Inchmarnock's secretary. Her ladyship is in her office.'

Catriona followed the girl along miles, it seemed, of polished floor until they reached the double doors of Flora's office.

'You know, even after all these years, I still find it hard to think of you as anybody other

193

than Dr Flora Currie,' she said as they hugged.

Flora laughed. 'I'll be Dr Flora now, old friend, and say that you're looking as if you haven't slept much lately.'

The story of Andrew and his perfidy spilled out; her unwillingness to share with Victoria who was so busy with her own child, her regret that a child who had been given everything should never seem to be satisfied.

Flora thought of the Mexican boy who had started life with so little and she wished that Alejandro and not Andrew had been Catriona's child as well as John's. How could two sons of the same father be so different?

'I suppose you have found him a good lawyer, Catriona?' Flora asked as she poured a second cup of hot, strong tea and added sugar.

'The best in Glasgow but Flora, part of me wants to let him rot. He has thrown everything back in our faces, all his life. Davie loved him and, as soon as he found that John and not Davie was his father, he changed.'

Or perhaps he reverted to his true nature. thought Flora, but she said nothing. 'You haven't told Victoria?'

'No, apart from her worry over wee Nancy, she's never really been that fond of Andrew. Goodness knows she tried and, even although she didn't have to, she's always given him half of any profits from the farm, although Eddie does all the work.'

'Catriona,' Flora began delicately. 'Did John make a will leaving the farm to Victoria?'

'No, he never made a will. Old Jock's will left everything to his legal heirs and Arbuthnott Boatman, he that was Jock's lawyer, says that meant first John and then John's legal heir and that would be Victoria.'

'Yes, it would,' smiled Flora and did not add that it would be Victoria unless John had a legal male heir and since his marriage to the Mexican girl was legal, he did have. Alejandro Alcantarilla-Medina was the real owner of Priory Farm.

She said nothing, of course. It was not her secret to divulge and Alejandro himself was unsure of what to do. He did not need or want the farm but whether he would like to be made known to his half sister or indeed to his half brother, he had not yet decided. For the moment he was content to study his beloved music and to share his most intimate thoughts with the old nun, Mother

Mercedes. Flora returned her full attention on her old friend.

'Doctors have lots of theories, Catriona, about why some children go bad, as it were and there are as many theories as there are doctors. Some say it's in the nature, some say it's how they're raised. You gave Andrew an idyllic childhood when many women would have rejected him because of circumstances...'

'Flora, do you think maybe unconsciously I saw John in him and that's what caused the trouble.'

'Nonsense. I don't think you and Davie thought of Andrew as other than Davie's from the moment he was born. Now don't distress yourself any more. There's enough to worry about with wee Nancy although I'm told that Victoria swears she's sensed movement.'

Catriona smiled. 'I watch her by the hour, Flora, and see nothing but Victoria rarely leaves her and she plays records all the time. Flora's persuaded her to play hit parade as well as all that Classical stuff. I mean wouldn't. "Oh, Johnny, oh Johnny" and "Three Little Fishes" be more likely to wake a wee lassie up than Beethoven?'

Flora thought of the boy who was possibly

Nancy's uncle playing Beethoven. Where did this love of music come from? 'Well, if my Jamie was asleep, Catriona, I think we'd have a better chance with the Edinburgh City Police Pipe Band.'

As she had hoped Catriona laughed naturally. Laughter, after all, is the best medicine.

Dr James Bains Sinclair loved his work. He was constantly exhausted, quite often hungry, and, of course, grossly underpaid but he was happy. London was very different from Dundee but he embraced the city, as much of it as he had time to find. He was constantly discovering wee things to tell his parents about, and he bought books and postcards for his mother and sister and his young friend, Nancy Welborn. He carried a note from her around in the breast of his smart officer's jacket.

Be warned, Jimmy, it read. *Don't look at any other women in London because I intend to marry you when I grow up.*

'If she grows up,' he thought now as he made his rounds. 'Please God, let her get well and she can marry whoever she chooses.' And then he laughed. 'Except me. I'm allergic to horses.'

He forgot Nancy and everyone else except his patients for the next few hours. Despite the chaos outside, inside the hospital the staff went about their duties calmly and professionally, wincing at the sound of the air raid warnings.

There was the all clear, possibly even a more horrifying sound.

'Well,' said Nurse Maggie Gordon, 'if they were planning a raid our boys in blue have scared them off again. Time for a cup of tea, Doctor?'

'Absolutely, Maggie. Tea I can dance on as my mother says.'

Maggie poured the dark brew into two mugs, heaped sugar into his and then added some condensed milk. 'I'd like to meet your mother some time,' she said gazing at him from over the top of the mug.

Jimmy looked at the shining undisciplined red curls and the big blue eyes gazing at him so innocently. 'It's Jimmy when we're off duty, Maggie, and maybe you will one day, meet my mother I mean. Fancy a weekend in Bonnie Scotland.'

'Goodness, Jimmy, aren't you a fast worker. A weekend in Scotland and we haven't even had tea at Lyons corner House. Shame on you.'

He smiled back at her. 'It's the war, Nurse. Even the best brought up lads have to cut corners. By the way, I'm off tomorrow lunchtime. How about a meal somewhere or a walk in the park. I never seem to get enough fresh air in London.'

'We could take sandwiches to the park, Jimmy. My mum bakes her own bread. Melts in the mouth.'

They smiled at one another, two young people taking the first steps towards a relationship. And then the air raid warning sounded again and they gulped the last mouthful of sustaining tea and hurried to their stations.

'Tomorrow, Maggie?'

'You have a date, Doctor.'

One plane, one single plane was limping across London on its way home. It had been hit and the pilot, who had had no instructions to target London, decided to jettison his bombs to lighten his load and facilitate his return journey.

The young doctor stood quietly in the middle of the ward listening. There was silence, the silence that was more frightening than the continued thud of pounding guns. At least that sound told you what was happening.

'Doc,' croaked a young sailor in the bed nearest the window, 'Doc, what's happening?'

Jimmy walked over to him and gently pushed the boy back against his pillows. 'It's nothing, Tom, go back to sleep.'

'I hate the silence, Doc, more than the guns. Hear that, that spluttering? That's a plane in trouble that is. It's just above us, Doc.'

The two young men looked up for one brief second and saw the world dissolve around them.

Neither felt anything.

Episode 9

'Come on, Nellie. It's ITMA on the wireless.'

'ITMA?' Nellie looked at her husband as if she did not understand a word he was saying.

'Aye, Nellie lass, your favourite programme. Tommy Handley.' Willie smiled encouragingly as if he was dealing with a young child or perhaps someone who was very, very seriously ill. 'Nellie, lass, it's Thursday. Remember Mrs Mopp and Colonel Chinstrap?'

Nellie looked up at him and smiled, a pale imitation of her former all enveloping grin. 'No my favourite programme, Willie, oor Jimmy's. Do you mind how he used tae run in. *The wireless, Mum, the wireless, switch on the wireless. Can I do yer now, sir?* He was good at the imitations, wasn't he, Willie?'

She did not move from her seat. In fact she very seldom moved from it and when she did, she moved around their cottage like one of them automatons he had seen at a fair. Put a penny in and it went through its wee programme and then collapsed again.

The cottage that she had turned, with hard work and love, into a comfortable welcoming home, was still clean and tidy but it no longer shone either with polish or the spirit of its mistress.

'I've it switched on, lass, and you'll be warm and comfy by the fire.'

Willie helped his wife to her feet and she went with him to the fireside. He kicked back the log that was threatening to fall on her lovely rag rug and settled his wife in her chair. 'I've a cup of tea made and some shortie Mrs Welborn sent down. I'm thinking they didnae have much of a Christmas either.'

Nellie said nothing but drank her tea and ate the shortbread. Last Christmas the shortbread, lighter and crisper, would have been her own but she had made few preparations this year for the holidays. Even their daughter had run out of patience with her mother's overwhelming grief and had gone back early to Edinburgh to bring in the New Year with her friends.

Willie listened to the programme but in the face of Nellie's silence he found his own occasional snort of laughter almost obscene; he turned off the wireless and they sat quietly, drinking the tea and smiling at one another politely as if they were strangers at a Church social.

'Nellie,' said Willie at last, 'it's near six months.'

She looked at him strangely. 'Six months, Willie, is it six months already?' she asked and her usually loving voice was heavy with sarcasm. 'Six months since my boy was killed, six years, sixty? Is that supposed tae make a difference?'

What could he say? He was no good with words, never had been.

'Nothing'll bring him back, Nellie, but I'm

still here and so is Mary Flora.'

She looked insultingly round the small warm room. 'I see you, Willie. Where's my daughter?'

'It was me sent her away, Nellie, for the New Year. She's a lassie and needs parties and fun.'

'Jimmy liked parties.'

'And he loved his sister and would be the first one to tell her to live, Nellie lass, no bury herself alive in her kitchen.'

She walked past him and left the room and he heard her steps on the stairs.

Willie Sinclair swore viciously for a moment. Then he dropped wearily back into his chair by the fire. Nellie had gone up to bed and left him. Never before had she turned her back on him.

Willie could not know it but circumstances up at the farm would help Nellie come to terms with her grief.

Nancy Welborn had been allowed home from the hospital on Christmas Eve. Her bones had healed but the injury to her brain would never heal properly. Nancy's body would age, but not her mind. She was a child but the happy child who had played and sang around the farm was gone for ever and a silent wraith had returned in her place.

'Her memory will improve,' the doctors had told them, 'but it will be a slow process and she will need constant care.'

On Christmas Day Nancy sat quietly like a slightly nervous guest and opened her presents and then, very carefully, wrapped them up again. She sat at the table and she ate her Christmas dinner and even pulled a cracker but she no longer giggled when her father put on the purple paper hat found in his cracker, and she did not put on the garish plastic ring that was in hers.

'Time, Victoria,' said Eddie. 'Give her time.'

Victoria tried to smile at her husband. We all need time, she thought as she looked from her injured daughter to her mother. Her brother, Andrew, was, she supposed, eating his Christmas dinner in prison in Glasgow but what her mother felt about that, Victoria could not tell. Catriona's face gave nothing away as she tried to cheer young Flora.

'Are you going to the church social on New Year's Eve, Flora? I think Flora Sinclair is going.'

'She's away back to Edinburgh, Gran. You'd think Nellie had fallen on her head. She sits all day like our Nancy.'

204

'Flora, what a terrible thing to say,' said Eddie while Victoria tried to hold back threatening tears.

'It's true, Daddy. Flora said her dad told her to go and have fun with her friends from College. Nellie's so ... so changed. She just sits, doesn't hear you when you speak to her.'

'Poor Nellie,' said Victoria. She had almost lost Nancy. She could *almost* understand what Nellie and Willie were going through. 'Try to understand, dear.'

'I understand perfectly, Mum. Nellie was so wrapped up in her precious Jimmy that she's forgotten she's got a daughter and a husband. Jimmy was Willie's son too and he was my friend.'

'I like Jimmy,' said Nancy and her family stared at her. It was the first full sentence she had uttered in six months.

In 1941 the Germans began the construction of a camp at Oswiecim in Poland. They translated its name into German. Auschwitz.

Professor Piaseczany had heard about it first in a letter from a Christian friend living in Lodz, the same friend who had tried so desperately to discover what had happened to Anneliese.

Soon it would be 1942 and, already, the world had heard about Auschwitz. 'Don't let them put my Anneliese there,' Emil prayed as he walked down the High Street in Dundee. He no longer knew to whom or what he prayed but prayer was a habit and habits are sometimes impossible to break.

He had almost bumped into Victoria before he saw her and since it was impossible to avoid her without being insufferably rude, he stopped and raised his hat.

'Mrs Welborn, how good to see you. Your daughter, she is well?'

Victoria had blushed a little when she first saw him. It had been months, months when despite herself he had filled her dreams and often her waking thoughts. She would be formal too. Formality made difficult situations easy.

'Professor, how very nice to see you.' The warmth of her smile left him in no doubt as to the sincerity of her greeting. 'My daughter is at home.' She said no more than that. It was still difficult to talk about the tragedy that was her little Nancy. 'And your daughter? Anneliese. Have you heard?'

'Nothing. In almost a year, nothing. All the Jews in our village were rounded up, rounded up like sheep or cows and transported like sheep or cows but I do not know where they took her.'

'Oh, Emil, I'm so sorry.' There, she had used his name. Don't do it, don't do it, her head warned her, but her heart spoke. 'I'm dying for a coffee. I was going up to Lamb's. Would you care to join me?' She could not take him to Elsie's even if Elsie had been in London instead of on a flying visit home.

He smiled and looked quickly up at a threatening sky. 'That would be pleasant,' he said. 'We can shelter from the rain, or will it be snow, do you think?'

He took her arm and they hurried to Reform Street and were soon seated at a small table, a pot of coffee or what passed for coffee in front of them.

'Can you bear to talk about it, Emil? Have you heard nothing?'

'She is not dead. She is all I have and so I would know, I think. The International Red Cross, they are trying to help and there are Jewish organisations also but so far she is not found. But she is not dead.'

He said that as if it were a mantra that he had to repeat for his sanity's sake. 'I am glad about your little girl, Victoria.'

'Her brain is damaged,' she said bluntly. 'She will never get better. She is there, Emil, in the room beside me but she is not there. Nancy exists inside herself. It's difficult to explain.'

'I'm so sorry,' he said and touched her hand.

She felt his touch in her heart. How could that be, but it was the same effect as a small electric shock.

'She's only been home for a few days and this is the first time I've left her but Eddie's good' – she blushed again as she said her husband's name – 'and Flora, my older girl. I needed some shopping for Hogmanay...'

'I also,' he said. 'I must buy the proper things, if I can. Whisky and bread, bread is easy, I think, and coal, I am told.'

'Your host won't expect these traditions, Emil.'

'I know. If I cannot find something more suitable I will give them my Beethoven records. It is all I have of any value.'

She smiled with genuine warmth. 'I've been so grateful that you introduced me to Beethoven, Emil. I played a record over and over to my daughter while she was in the coma. She did seem to like it but Flora says she prefers "Deep in the Heart of Texas."'

He laughed. 'A Philistine, but who cares. She is healthy and happy.'

'Yes, healthy and, I hope, happy.'

'Keep her happy, Victoria.'

'We try. I think we neglected her a little while Nancy was so ill. It's so difficult to be in two places at the same time and my ... friend' – she had been about to say, my cleaning lady but Nellie was more, so much more – 'my friend, Nellie, lost her son in an air raid, and she has been ignoring her daughter because her heart is broken. He was a doctor, a lovely boy...' She could not continue.

'We are all victims, Victoria, and those of us who are left must help each other. This simple cup of coffee, this sharing bad news and good with a friend, has helped me.'

'Me too. I have missed ... our ... friend-ship.'

'I too. Maybe next year, Victoria, we can go to a concert. Our cares will not go away but we can share them perhaps.'

'I'd like that.'

Emil paid the bill and they walked out into the crisp cold day. The magnificent Grecian structure of the High School stood proudly on their right and beside it, the imposing beauty of the Art Galleries.

'This street is so lovely, but especially in the spring,' said Victoria.

'I walked from my lodging. The sky is so clear, I could see the whole picture; the Law, St. Mary's Tower, Balgay Hill with behind all the hills of Perthshire and before the astonishing beauty of the Tay. Who can believe in Auschwitz on such a day?'

She touched his hand for a second. 'We'll defeat tyranny, Emil, and we'll bring your daughter home.'

Singapore fell to the Japanese in February, the King, so it was said, painted a Plimsoll line on the bath tubs in Buckingham Palace, Elsie Morrison, who had always been 'up' on the latest in clothes and make up, used soot to darken her eyebrows, and Jamie Fotheringham got his wings.

'God help the enemy,' said his father in a Christian if not particularly patriotic way.

'God help his friends,' said his more worldly wise mother.

But her Jamie was probably just the kind of devil me care young man for whom the Air Force was looking. He was brave but not foolhardy; he was fascinated by everything to do with flight and he had learned not to complain too loudly when his feet were cold. The Air Force had discovered other skills his parents knew nothing about; tolerating cold feet was not one of them.

Stationed in Fife, he was able to see his mother quite often and, of course, he got to know Connie Faraday. Whenever possible they went to dances at his Station and sometimes Jamie was able to stay for the night in a tiny room at the very top of Inchmarnock House. His family owned the house, his brother had been born and had died there and the heir slept, quite happily, in what had been a maid's room in the attics. If there were ghosts in the old house they did not intrude on the young airman's sleep.

In May he celebrated the Government's postponement of plans to ration fuel by driving Connie through to Glasgow to see Alejandro play at a Red Cross concert.

The newspapers made much of the 'Mexican' virtuoso.

'They won't think you quite so marvellous when they discover you're a plain old Scot, Xandro, old boy,' laughed Jamie later as they waited for a table at Rogano, the fish restaurant which was quite near his college. 'Don't know what it is about the Scots, but they're terrified of one of their own getting above himself. You'll have to watch out for that.'

'Can a boy brought up in an orphanage ever "get above himself" as you say, Jamie?' asked Xandro and then turned his devastating grey-blue eyes on Connie. 'Why do you waste your time with old Jamie, Connie?'

'I have to; his mother is my boss.'

Jamie ignored this. 'How are you getting along with all the legal stuff? Dad says he's made a few introductions for you.'

'He's been marvellous and the college is helpful too. I think, very soon, I will be given a British birth certificate. My name is legally Cameron. It always was; only my grandfather and my uncles hated my father so much, they just conveniently left his name off everything but his marriage certificate.'

'And the family, the Camerons, Menmuirs etceteras?'

'How can I burst in on them? Mrs Menmuir's son, my half-brother, is in prison. Mrs Welborn's daughter is ill, I believe. This is not the time to say, "Hello, I'm your little brother and the girl's uncle." Can you be a half uncle.'

Jamie looked at his old friend. 'I'd be quite happy to find you were my half-brother, Xandro.'

'For once Jamie is right,' said Connie. 'I

think that to discover there is a half-brother would be very exciting.'

'They may not like the contrast,' said Alejandro and then blushed furiously when he saw his friends had misinterpreted his remark. 'I meant only that my skin is darker and my hair and even my language is different, not that I was a better person.'

'Would you like to know them as family, Xandro? A half-brother inside is hardly going to do wonders for your international career?' Jamie brought up something that Xandro had never considered.

'If I play well enough my family connections will hardly matter, but, for me, to have a sister who shares my blood and a brother, even if he has made a mistake, these are the important issues.'

'And the farm? Mrs Menmuir can't inherit if you're your father's legitimate son.'

Xandro had many plans in his head and none of them had anything to do with a few acres of ground but as yet he was unable to tell even Jamie about them.

'I have interest in seeing this farm, Jamie. You can understand and you, Connie, how important it is to feel that you belong somewhere. For ten years I had only Sister Mercedes whom I loved but I was not allowed to show my affection and perhaps, when I was a child, I did not know that I loved her. Surely for any human being to be able to say, *here I belong,* is paramount?'

'Studying music is where you belong, old thing,' said Jamie. The conversation was becoming much too sentimental for him. Old Xandro might want to think he was a Scot but there was an awful lot of warm Latino about him. 'But, if you really want to get to know your relatives, Mum's a good friend of Mrs Menmuir and probably the best person to tell her about you. There's nothing to be ashamed of, after all. The Camerons were divorced long before your parents married.'

'I can wait, Jamie. I have waited over twenty years already. Perhaps if I visit you in Fife, then I can meet my sister, but for now, the most important thing in my life is to be acknowledged as a subject of the King.'

They stopped being solemn and returned to being youngsters with not a thought beyond the next meal. Then Xandro returned to College, Connie to her hospital and Jamie to his base where in July he began to fly Mosquitos. He had trained in Blenheim Bombers which had actually taken sheer brute strength as well as brains to fly

214

and he loved the new light aircraft. His squadron was in the Royal Air Force Coast Command under the command of Air Chief Marshal Sir Sholto Douglas. Jamie thought he might, one day, aspire to Sir Sholto's position but for now he was content to fly, to feel that he was part of the great war effort. The airforce would win the war. He knew it. All the others with him knew it. They just had to persuade the enemy.

He could not tell his parents of the adrenalin rush when he actually had complete control of a plane in the air, when he knew that only his skill and Lady Luck were between him and disaster. What was a plane but a few pieces of metal and wood with, a few feet from his cold feet, a full fuel tank?

'God must feel like this when He looks down and sees His world spread out below him,' thought Jamie irreverently and then prayed for forgiveness for his blasphemy.

The voice screeched in his ear. 'Do you see it, Jamie? That's Milan straight ahead. There's anti-aircraft guns down there with your name on them *and* your blooming title in case they get the wrong guy. In and out, laddie, and back to base in time for Bovril.'

The RAF was conducting round the clock

215

raids on that triangle in the North of Italy bounded by the industrial centres of Milan, Genoa, and Turin. The biggest raid on Italy of the war so far had begun in Turin just a few days before but there was still impassioned fighting from below. That night, however, the anti-aircraft gunners did not have Jamie's name. They stared up through smoke rimmed eyes.

'Next time,' they yelled into the sky. 'Next time.'

'You're seeing quite a bit of my son, Connie,' said Lady Inchmarnock.

'Yes, Ma'am.'

'And young Alejandro?'

'Do you mind, Lady Inchmarnock?' asked Connie as she tried not very successfully, to balance chits to be signed with chits to be filed and letters to be signed with letters and memos still to be typed.

'Not all, my dear. It's just that I think of Jamie as a mere boy.'

'We're friends, Ma'am, but I have to say they grow up quickly in the airforce.'

Both women were quiet as they thought, in different ways, about the young men. Connie knew what Lady Inchmarnock did not and that was that her beloved son was no longer on his base in Fife but *somewhere in the European Theatre.*

'We hope to see Casablanca soon,' said Connie at last, 'If it gets up to Scotland.'

'It's super. Lord Inchmarnock and I saw it in London.' Flora reached across and relieved Connie of some of the papers which she put down on her blotter and began to sort out.

'What on earth would you have done for a living if there hadn't been a war?'

Connie flushed but she no longer felt afraid of her boss. Lady Inchmarnock knew that she worked hard. She was not the neatest secretary in the world but the work was always done – eventually – and besides, she did much more. In a hospital of this kind, someone happy to sit by an injured man's bedside was someone to be treasured and Connie was a treasure.

'I'd have made a debut in a fabulously over-priced gown, gone from one boozy party to the next, met some pimply youth and married him, I suppose. I wouldn't have had your courage, Ma'am.'

Connie knew not only that her boss was one of the country's first fully qualified doctors but that she had gone against family wishes to achieve her aims.

'I'm not sure that it took courage, my dear. I was doing what I wanted to do and – possibly – I'm not sure but possibly, if the man I loved had loved me in return, I might have married him then instead of twenty years later. Are you doing what you want to do?'

Connie thought hard. 'I had no great desire to be a secretary, if that's what you mean, but I burned to help. Is that enough, Lady Inchmarnock?' She was not talking about the letters.

'Yes, dear, and you are helping, in so many ways, Connie. The doctors and nurses tell me, you know, about all the extras.'

Connie shook her head. 'In my own time. Some of the men never get visitors, you know. If my brother was in hospital some-where and the family couldn't get to him, it would help to know someone was visiting. I despair sometimes about the war. The Germans slaughtered all the Jews in Warsaw this summer. How can we fight that kind of evil? Will the war ever end?'

Flora had been reading some letters but at the note of desperation in the girl's voice she looked up. 'Connie, you're over tired. I work you too hard. Look at all these memos.' She moved round her desk and put her hand on the girl's shoulder. 'Now listen to me. Doctor's orders. Take a few days off and go and see your mother. I thought I might have a little break too and invite my old landlady over here for a few days. If I desperately need secretarial help, there are several patients who would love to do something useful.'

That was quite true and when Catriona Menmuir drove up to Inchmarnock House a young man in pyjamas and a dressing gown invited her in.

'A temporary secretary, Catriona. Don't tell her I said so but he's so much more efficient than my dear Connie. I may well hire him when this war is over.' She saw the signs of strain on the older woman's face. 'Come on, Catriona, I'll take you up to your room and then we'll have a nice cup of tea.'

'I don't want to burden you with my problems, Flora,' said Catriona softly as they sat balancing porcelain plates on their starched laps.

'Is Andrew well?'

'Yes, but I can tell, I'm his mother, and there's no remorse there. He's sorry, but sorry he got caught. I've told him about wee Nancy. He played with her, Flora; he loved her when she was a toddler. What changes them? He said, Victoria can afford the best doctors. Not, how awful, Mum, poor wee lamb or anything like that, just Victoria can afford the best doctors.'

'It's all bravado, Catriona. Try not to let it worry you. How is Victoria?'

Catriona thought. She sipped her tea and held out her cup for more. 'I'm worried about her. She leaves Nancy with Eddie quite often. Of course she needs a break but...' Should she tell Flora? Oh, dear God, she had to tell someone. 'I think she's seeing another man.'

Eddie Welborn thought so too. He watched his wife drive away and his heart was breaking. Was this the day when she would not return? Since the New Year, almost, dear God, almost a year, there had been a change in Victoria. It was a change that was for the better, of course. She was happier and no longer seemed to be quite so strained as she had been.

'Jimmy's house.'

Eddie turned. Nancy was beside him. He had not heard her and he was startled. She moved very quietly these days, no longer his noisy laughing daughter who had clattered up and down stairs and banged doors.

'All right, sweetheart. I'll walk down with you. You'll need a coat, Nancy. It's cold.'

Obediently she went back into the house with him and sat quietly on the edge of her bed while he looked through her wardrobe for a warm sweater and a jacket. Before the accident she would have spurned the jacket. 'It's not cold, Daddy, it's fresh.'

He found a red woollen sweater that Catriona had knitted for her granddaughter. Nancy loved bright colours. She helped him pull it on over her blouse and then she stood up and let him help her on with her bright blue jacket.

'There, you'll be nice and warm now, sweetheart.'

'Jimmy's house.'

He walked before his daughter down the stairs across the hall and outside. He waited patiently while she opened the gate and closed it behind her.

'No cows,' she said.

'No cows,' he agreed.

Once when she had been quite small Nancy had left the gate to the garden open and several cows, on their way to the milking shed, had wandered in and churned up Victoria's garden. The incident had not been mentioned for years but now Nancy remembered it every time she walked in or out of the garden.

Gate closed, they walked on down the farm road stopping every now and then to look over a hedge or a fence. Eddie talked to Nancy constantly since he was positive that this was a help to her continued improvement. She answered him sometimes, rarely in sentences but he cherished the communication. Something was going on behind those childlike eyes. He knew it. One day the door that was locked would be opened. He knew it.

'There are no leaves on the trees now, Nancy.' She stopped obediently and looked at the trees.

'No leaves,' she said.

'Why sweetheart, why no leaves?'

'No leaves.'

'It's because it's winter again and the trees are sleeping.'

'Jimmy's house,' she said but this time with pleasure because they were there.

Willie was in the garden tidying. There were few vegetables left, one or two cabbages, but no Brussels sprouts.

'Hello, Nancy,' he said and his eyes smiled at her.

222

'Jimmy's house,' she told him and he opened the gate for her.

'You'll come in and have a cup of tea, Boss?'

'No, Willie. If you'll bring her home in an hour or two I'll get some paperwork done.'

The door to the cottage opened and he saw Nellie. She was thin and pale and her hair was quite grey but it was almost the old Nellie again. 'Hello, pet,' she called. 'Have you come to tea? Bring Daddy in then,' she said stepping back into the cottage.

Nancy turned to her father. 'Jimmy's house.'

Eddie looked at the little cottage where his Nancy was always welcome. 'You go in and see Nellie, sweetheart. I have some paper-work to do.'

She almost ran down the path to Nellie who closed the door behind her.

Willie straightened up and the two men looked at each other.

'How's it going, Willie?'

'They're grand for one another, boss. Nellie's accepted the boy's gone but Nancy's still waiting on him. They look at photies and his books. Does Nellie good and your wee lass nae harm. Oor lass has a fellow that she's bringing hame at the New

223

Year. Things can only get better, Boss.'

'You're right, Willie,' said Eddie as he turned to begin his lonely walk home. 'Things can only get better.'

Episode 10

Alejandro Alcantarilla-Medina was delighted with his Christmas present. It was an officially signed document which told anyone who wanted to know that he was a British citizen.

He hugged the letter to him and wanted to rush to the nearest telephone to let Jamie know, and Lord and Lady Inchmarnock, and Connie, all the people who mattered to him.

First he wrote a long letter to Sister Mercedes. He told her of his love for her and his appreciation of the education she had given him.

... dearest little Madre, how often I long to see you, to hear you scold ... 'for my own good'.

When I struggled with the English language at Fettes I did not really appreciate your insistence that I learn to speak French, but that lovely

224

language has been so useful in my study of music.

Then he told her about his joy in his studies and of his plans for the future. He knew that she might not agree with him but she would support him.

Soon, Madre mia, the whole world will be at war, not only Europe. Pray for me ... why do I ask? I know that you do. If I am one of the countless casualties, remember that I love you and will always be your,

Alejandro

When term ended he accepted the Inchmarnocks' invitation to join them for Christmas. He managed to get a train from Glasgow to Newport-on-Tay and he walked from the station down the brae to the great house hidden in the trees where Flora Fotheringham was working as hard as possible so that she could steal away for a few days to join her husband in Edinburgh to celebrate the holiday season.

'Look, Connie,' he said as he opened the door of her tiny office. 'It's official; I'm as British as you are.'

She hugged him and then laughed. 'Only your eyes are British, Xandro, but don't worry, I won't tell a soul.'

Since Lady Inchmarnock was on the

225

wards with a visiting consultant they chatted about their plans for Christmas. Xandro was not yet ready to talk of anything else. The Inchmarnocks first and Jamie.

'You just caught me, you know, Xandro. I'm leaving for London tonight. My brother's got leave and we're all so excited and longing to see him.'

Xandro smiled. As far as he knew no-one's eyes had ever sparkled with excitement at the thought of seeing him come home. After all, where was home, an orphanage in Mexico, Fettes, the Inchmarnock houses? No, no, it was a little farmhouse in Angus. He had to see it this year.

He asked Flora if she could effect an introduction.

She smiled at him. 'Xandro dear, of course I can take you out to Priory Farm but what will I say? How will I introduce you? This is Alejandro Medina; he owns your home.'

'Lady Flora, just to see the house and the land from where my father came is enough. I wish I could explain it to you.'

Flora looked at the young man who was almost as dear to her as her own son. 'I do understand, dear. Why don't I ring Catriona Menmuir? After all she and your father had been divorced for years; she's not likely to...'

She stopped, unsure as to how to continue.

'To resent me,' he finished for her. 'Lady Flora, they need not,' he said again. 'I have my music and there is my mother's family in Mexico who think I am no longer to be despised. But my father who died before I was born came from this farm. I have, I believe, a right to see it.'

'Of course you do, Xandro,' said Lady Inchmarnock and she reached for the telephone.

Victoria was surprised that her mother wanted to see her so urgently.

'Mum, I have so much to do before Christmas. Why are you being so mysterious? Can't it wait till you get here?'

'No, it can't. Your future, Eddie's future, the girls. It could depend on this.'

'Good heavens, Mum, you can't say something like that to me on the telephone and not explain. What on earth is it? Are you ill? Is it Andrew? Have you heard from him?'

Catriona laughed but it was not a pleasant sound. 'Oh, Victoria, I never thought I would ever say again that your brother Andrew is the least of my worries. Do you mind on thon Mexican boy Jamie Fotheringham brought to Davy's funeral?'

'Yes, vaguely. I wasn't thinking.'

227

'No, neither was I but it turns out he's your brother too.'

Victoria had been standing in the hall, hoping that she could quickly finish the call and return to her baking. Now she slumped into a chair and for a quick moment put her head down between her knees. Then she sat up. She could cope. Always.

'What are you trying to say, Mother?'

Catriona told her and then burst into tears.

Much later that evening when Nancy was peacefully asleep and Mary Flora had gone into Dundee to meet up with some old schoolfriends, Victoria broke the news to Eddie.

She looked at him as he sat trying to comprehend the enormity of what she was telling him. He had aged. Why had she not noticed? Because of my worry over Nancy, she told herself and then because Victoria had always tried to be honest with herself she admitted that she had been too full of her growing friendship with Emil Piase-czany to notice anything. Even now, with this sword of Damocles hanging over them, the very thought of her dear Emil filled her with joy.

'Are you telling me,' asked Eddie at last,

'that the farm I've slaved on and over for the last twenty odd years belongs to some Mexican piano player. Victoria, we have a daughter who will never grow up mentally. She'll need constant care for the rest of her life, and what am I supposed to do? Soldiering and farming are all I have ever understood and I'm too old for the soldiering. And before you start, don't go on about the success of your mother's garage. Yes, it has been a success, Catriona is a remarkable woman and I love and respect her, but the war won't be good for garages, Victoria. A car won't run without petrol. There'll be rationing and where will Catriona's profits be then? We'll find ourselves with medical bills, university fees – and no income.'

Victoria swallowed hard. It could happen. The worst *could* happen. It had happened to others. Why not to them?

'Flora says he wants only to see the land. I think the mother's people were rich. He doesn't want to take our home, Eddie but if it's his by right...' Then she came to an irrevocable decision. 'For Nancy I'll fight.'

'But not for me?'

She flushed an ugly red. 'Don't be so melodramatic, Eddie. You're my husband. I only meant that ... oh dear, we don't even

229

know yet if he is the rightful owner. I'll need, we'll need to speak to Mr Boatman. He'll know what my grandfather's will said.'

'And your brother?'

'We don't know where Andrew went when he was released.'

'I meant the Mexican. This handsome, talented new half-brother of yours.'

Victoria sat back slowly. Her brother. How wonderful to have a brother with whom one could share; a brother to laugh with, to talk with about the sadness and joy of Nancy and the growing and developing of the young woman, Mary. They were his nieces and he was a classical musician. Emil had taught her to love and appreciate beautiful music but maybe, deep inside, there was some gene she shared with the Mexican boy and Emil had merely awakened that gene.

Do I want to see him, to know him? I don't know, I don't know. I'm afraid.

'We could invite him to see the farm; no harm in that.'

'Pity he couldn't see it the way it was before I spent twenty years on it,' said Eddie bitterly and Victoria mourned for his lost youth. When had her Eddie grown bitter?

'The war won't last for ever and we'll have a share of the garage, Eddie,' she reminded him but that was the wrong thing to say. He got up and left the room.

Victoria cooked and cleaned for Xandro's visit and Eddie made sure the farm and steading had never looked tidier, not an easy thing to do in Angus in winter. He was a farmer and he wanted his land to look its best. He could not do anything else and Victoria was grateful.

Flora brought Catriona and Xandro and Victoria found herself remembering the night when the young Dr Flora Currie had driven out to tell them of Andrew's birth. Now she brought another, younger brother.

She looked at Xandro. He was taller than Eddie, very slim and very dark but his eyes ... she had seen eyes like that before. They were the same as those of her beloved grandfather. Could a man with eyes like that take her beloved farm from her? She had to be careful, to tread warily.

To her amazement she heard herself say, 'Welcome home, Xandro,' and she held out her hands to him.

He took her hands in his and she saw the long strong pianist's fingers, beautiful strong hands. He could not speak but smiled at her.

'I like horses. Come see.' It was Nancy

who had come with Eddie to see who was in the car.

She held out her hand, not to her grandmother or Lady Inchmarnock, but to Xandro. He smiled at the girl. 'I like horses too,' he said and took her hand.

'Two sentences,' said Victoria. 'Eddie, that was two sentences.'

They stood and watched as, hand in hand, Xandro and Nancy walked down the farm road to the paddock.

'Horses,' said Eddie. 'That's the first time she's said anything about horses since the accident. Why, Flora, why would she suddenly speak to a complete stranger?'

'I have no idea, Eddie dear,' said Flora. 'We know so little of the working of the brain. Perhaps she was ready, perhaps something about Xandro triggered a response. He used to ride with Jamie and then his family are land owners in Mexico, descended from Spanish conquerors, all magnificent horsemen. Who knows? Just accept, my dear.'

They walked slowly along behind Xandro and Nancy and Eddie and Victoria listened to their daughter chattering, yes, chattering to a complete stranger. It was the conversation of an artless child and Victoria knew in her heart that this was all they would ever hear from Nancy but she was talking, not merely saying odd words – but talking.

At the gate to the field Xandro turned and smiled at Victoria. 'We have so much in common, Nancy and I. Perhaps one day you will let me play for her. Mrs Menmuir has a piano, I believe, and music is a great bridge, Victoria. May I call you, Victoria?'

'Of course. I am your half-sister, after all.'

'All my life I have had no one who belonged to me,' he said with a slight smile. 'Even a half is wonderful.'

She smiled into his beautiful grey blue eyes, eyes that were the colour of water breaking over rocks in a pool, her father's eyes, but also old Jock Cameron's. 'I've made tea. Come and I'll show you the house and the room where our father was born.'

She took Nancy's other hand and with the others behind them they returned to the farmhouse.

It was too soon, Victoria felt, to talk about the future. Perhaps he would ask for a share in the farm, perhaps he was its rightful owner. Today it was good just to find a brother, to see the joy in her daughter's eyes as she discovered a new uncle. But that uncle could take her very home ... no, no,

233

she must wait and hope.

Xandro did not tell them, for first he would have to tell Jamie and the Inchmarnocks, but already he had filed an image of the farm and its family into a special place in his mind. It would be there to draw comfort from in the dark days ahead.

'What's a plimsoll line, Willie?'

Willie looked up from his paper and smiled at his wife. She was almost her old self again, almost. Spending so much time looking after wee Nancy had helped her. Nellie needed to know that she herself was needed. 'I need you, Nellie,' he wanted to say but he had never learned how to say things like that. Instead he said, 'It's a line painted round the keel of a ship so the captain kens how much weight it's carrying... I think there was this fella called Plimsoll aboot a hundred years ago and he said they was putting too much in Merchant ships and that sailing them was dangerous so they painted this line so you could tell if there was too much on board.'

'Then why does the king want me to paint one roon my bath? It's no sailing anywhere that I've heard.'

Victoria and Eddie had bought two cast

iron bath tubs at a Country House roup. One, with water plumbed in, was in the 'Bathroom' at Priory Farm and the second, even without running water, reposed in isolated splendour waiting for the modernisation of Angus at Nellie and Willie's cottage. Filling it from the range nearly killed Willie's back on Saturday nights but Nellie liked 'having a bath' and he would have carried hot water a lot farther than up the stairs for his Nellie.

'I dinnae understand these things, Nellie love. It seems that if we jist put a few inches of hot water in the bath on a Saturday instead filling it up and wallowing in it, we're helping win the war.'

'Good enough for me,' said Nellie and left the room.

Willie sat for a while trying to concentrate once again on the newspaper but he could not stop thinking about his wife and the Plimsoll line. Nellie hadn't been holding a pot of green paint in her hand when she'd been standing at the door, had she?

It was no use. He folded the paper, put it on the table, and went off after his wife. Yes, indeed, he could smell paint.

In the bathroom he found Nellie on her knees on the floor. Around the bottom of the deep iron bath tub she was painting a slightly wavy green line. Since the bath stood on iron feet she had continued her line across the legs and he saw, his heart almost bursting with happiness, that she had painted the toe nails of each great iron foot too. It was garish and at the same time the most beautiful job of painting he had ever seen in his life.

'I like the toe nails, love,' he said. 'You should maybe do your own and then what would our lassie say.'

'She'd be fair jealous,' smiled Nellie and continued along to the end of the bath.

He watched her with a huge grin, that she could not see, on his face.

'There,' she said triumphantly when she was finished. 'We're winning this war, Willie.'

'Right enough. There's jist one wee thing, Nellie love.'

She looked at him, waiting.

He could control his laughter no longer. 'Tell me this, Admiral. When you're stark naked, sitting in your bath, how can ye tell that you're up tae or over or under your Plimsoll line?'

He enjoyed the dawning realisation on her expressive face. 'Are you telling me, Willie

Sinclair, that the line's supposed tae be inside the bath.'

He saw the raised paint brush and turned to run for safety.

'I'll paint a plimsoll line on you, Willie Sinclair, if I get my hands on you and then you'll aye ken how much water you're sitting in.'

Her voice followed him downstairs.

He reached the safety of the kitchen and closed the door in case she came pounding down after him but there was silence from the stairs and he stood leaning against the door and laughed a little and cried a little too. Jimmy, their only son, was dead and nothing would ever make up for that but his Nellie was home again. The real Nellie had retreated into some private world when the boy went but wee Nancy Welborn and her problems had helped to draw her back and now the King, God bless him, and his plimsoll line.

'She can paint plimsoll lines wherever she fancies,' decided Willie. 'But I wish I'd had my bath afore she got started. She's got the bathroom that wet it'll take a month tae dry.'

He went to his chair by the fire and picked up his newspaper and a half-hour or so later

Nellie joined him.

'I'll get started on my Christmas baking, Willie, soon as I get my hands clean. Oor lassie will have her mammy's shortbread this New Year. I'm no saying Victoria's a bad baker but she's no a patch on her mother.'

'Richt enough, Nellie love, but tell me, afore you go, what do you think of this new turn of events.'

'You mean the foreign laddie? Victoria says he's the spit of auld Jock Cameron and if he's like him in nature too, it'll be fine.'

'Auld Jock, from what I hear, kent the value of his land.'

'And you think the foreign laddie will want a wee farm in Angus. It was willed tae Victoria so he can want.'

'You're wrong, Nellie. Word is it was willed tae John and then tae John's heir. That *was* Victoria but John Cameron was legally married tae the wee lassie in Mexico. Their boy comes first, then Victoria.'

Nellie stopped on her way to the scullery and turned round. 'You mean he could evict them?'

'I suppose he could, legally. The Priory's a guid ferm, worth a bit of money.'

'And here's Mrs Menmuir near ruined herself paying off all the trouble Andrew got hissel into. Some families really do get mair not their share, Willie. I'll make you a nice cup of tea and a bit cake. Then I'll start on my Black Bun for Hogmanay.'

'And Clootie Dumplin, Nellie love?'

She smiled. 'Clootie Dumplin? There's a war on, Willie Sinclair, and if you want dumplings and black bun then you'd best go and teach some of yer hens tae pit cracks in their shells! The shops don't want cracked eggs. Somebody on the farm'll jist have to use them up.'

He could hear her laughing to herself as she bustled around. There would still be black days; the pain would never go but it would ease. They had their daughter and they had, thank God, found one another again. One day, perhaps, he would manage to be more like Nellie and contrive to find pity for others in spite of his own grief.

Emil Piaseczany could not bear the thought of another Christmas with no news of his daughter. Despite his self control and self discipline his mind continued to torture him with pictures of what life in a concentration camp must be like for his little Anneliese. To make the images even more unbearable he found himself remembering

239

her childhood. He saw her helping to decorate the house for the Holy season, helping her mother and the cook bake all the special dishes. He saw her whirling around in a green velvet party dress, her shining hair escaping from its ribbons, her lovely face animated by joy.

He had tried everything he could think of to get news of her. He wrote letters, long loving letters telling her about Dundee, its river, its history and its people.

...*such a lovely people, my Anneliese. The more they have nothing, the more they give it away. Just wait until you come. No-one will say – who is this Polish Jew? Why should we take her, feed her, love her? They will say, here is a human being and what we have, we will share with her, and while she is so thin, she shall have the bigger share.*

He could not post the letters because he did not know where she was. Emil looked at the last long loving letter and, with a cry of unbearable pain, he crumpled it up and threw it in the waste basket. He had made a decision, one that he had been dissuaded from making time after time but now he was determined.

The first person who should know of his plans was Victoria.

He was in love with Victoria. There he had admitted it to himself. Her friendship had kept him sane but friendship was no longer enough – he remembered their stolen kisses. He wanted, he wanted, no, Victoria was a married woman and he could not destroy a marriage. Too much was being needlessly, heedlessly destroyed and it would take more than his lifetime to rebuild civilisation.

For the past six months he had been meeting Victoria at Elsie's apartment and each knew that it was a dangerous thing to do. They watered the plants, they listened to music, they kissed, oh such sweet forbidden kisses that reminded him that he was a man not a machine, and they talked, mainly about their fears for their daughters. Would either girl ever grow up? Nancy's mind had stopped forever on the day of her accident and his Anneliese? She would grow up. She must.

'I have a new experience for you today, my friend,' he said deliberately when they met just before Christmas. 'It is Fidelio, the only opera that Beethoven ever wrote. It is my gift to you. The music, of course, is sublime but it is the story, Victoria. It is about a woman who loves her husband so much that she dresses up as a prison guard and goes to find him. She lets nothing and no-one stand in her way. He lies in a cell dreaming of her, his angel, and at the end they are reunited. It is the story of the power of love, of faithfulness. We will play only one record today and you will take the others home.'

Victoria sat, her face pale, and watched his dear face as he bowed over the old gramophone. She saw his long fingers tremble slightly as they gently lowered the record onto the base. She knew what he was doing and she felt that she could not bear it. He was saying goodbye.

For a moment she wondered if it would do any good to throw herself into his arms, to offer to go with him wherever he was going, to leave everything, Eddie, Nancy, Mary Flora, the farm. The farm. Once the land had been everything. Now it was not enough. She could walk away from it without a backward glance but she could not leave her daughters. Her husband? Oh, what did she feel for her husband? Old feelings lay dead or were they buried under a weight of pain and worry. And her mother? Could she leave her mother especially now that Andrew, released from prison, had disappeared into some underworld that his family, she and his mother, could scarcely imagine. No point in asking why, why? She had to be there, didn't she, to help Catriona through this latest in a series of tragedies.

'I want to think only of myself for a while but could I? Can anybody do that? Would I really want to live like that? It was enough for Andrew and where did his selfishness lead him?'

She loved Emil Piaseczany and it was a different one from the love she had shared with Eddie. That had been peaceful, friendly. She knew that if she gave in to her love for Emil, its power could tear her apart. Was she prepared for that? Would she even be given the chance to find out, for Emil was already gone from her. Before she had found him, she had lost him.

She bowed her head so that he could not see her tears and she listened to the Overture.

He did not sit beside her.

They sat so intensely aware of one another and the music and when the first record finished they still sat and this time Victoria raised her head and looked at him.

'Emil, my dear?'

His sweet sad face looked back at her. 'Don't do this to us, Victoria. Do you know how difficult it is to sit here with you, wanting only to hold you and love you and to know that integrity demands that I leave you?'

She could bear it no longer. She rose from the seat and threw herself into his arms and he held her away for him and then, with a muffled groan, he clasped her to him and began to cover her face, her hair, with kisses.

'Victoria,' he murmured. 'Victoria.'

'Emil, my dearest,' she responded to his kisses. 'I love you. I have loved you from the first moment. Nothing else matters. Nothing.'

She forgot husband, child, farm, family. Nothing mattered but this overwhelming love that she had not sought but which had come to her and which must be joyously accepted, anguish and joy in equal measure. Or was anguish to have the larger part?

Emil, older, wiser, more used to suffering, came to his senses. Gently he disengaged himself and pushed her away.

'I want you to go, Victoria, now,' he said. 'I will tidy the music and lock the door. The key will be at the university. Just ask there, dear friend.' He smiled and it was a smile of unutterable sadness and sweetness. 'I am going to find my daughter. Don't ask me how because I do not know and what I do know I may not tell you. One day I will bring my Anneliese back to Dundee and then, maybe, we will meet again.'

He stood up and deliberately walked to the window where he stood in the darkness looking out. Victoria raised her hand as if to touch him, then turned, took her coat from the stand near the door and let herself out.

A week later she forced herself to go to the university. Someone's radio was playing. She heard the new hit, White Christmas, sung by the American heart throb, Bing Crosby. Nancy loved that song.

May your days be merry and bright...

A secretary handed Victoria an envelope with the key. There was also a note.

I love you as I have only ever loved one woman before but I cannot and will not ask you to leave all that is dear for me. The knowledge of you will sustain me in the months ahead. I hope you will play the Beethoven and think fondly of your own,

Fidelio

'Give that to me again.'

'Alejandro Alcantarilla-Medina.'

'You sure you're on our side, mate?'

245

Xandro laughed. 'I am but you're right. The name is a handful.' He thought of his parents' marriage certificate. 'Does Alexander Cameron sound better? That's almost the beginning and end of my full name. We'll just cut out the bits in the middle.'

The young Flying Officer looked carefully at the papers and then handed them back and smiled. 'Welcome to the Air Force, Sandy.'

Sandy Cameron. It could not be better. Sandy was Lord Inchmarnock's name and was easier to pronounce than Xandro, and perhaps using it was a way of thanking Lord Inchmarnock for all his kindnesses. He had not really understood Xandro's determination to prove his citizenship and then to, seemingly, throw away his career by joining up. He had, however, been supportive all the months that Xandro had been doing his basic training and after that, he had pulled whatever strings he still held so that he was able to get into the courses he needed.

And now, quietly, behind the scenes he had pulled the biggest string of all. Xandro had trained as a navigator only so that he could fly with Jamie. He could not tell Lord Inchmarnock that he had a deep seated feeling that Jamie needed him, just as he had needed Jamie during all those years at Fettes.

'I'll be there to look after him and maybe there will be some way, apart from playing Lady Flora's favourite sonatas, in which Sandy Cameron can help these friends, my family.'

Under which name he would re-enrol at the Academy of Music was another matter. They had said they would take him back and they had told him that on the day the news had arrived of two former students killed in action. But fine musicians were being killed on all sides. War didn't ask the value of its victims; death was indiscriminate and everyone was of value.

'Why do you want to be involved, Xandro?' a colleague had asked. 'Why didn't you wait until after this mess to get your birth certificate. You could sit out the war in Glasgow and be there for all the opportunities that will come. You're a fool.'

Perhaps that was how the world would see it. But as Sandy Cameron walked across the parade ground he knew that for him it was the right, the only decision. He had seen where his paternal roots were. One day he would return to Mexico, to see his beloved Mother Mercedes, perhaps to meet this

Don Jose Luis who said he was his uncle.

'You can wait, Uncle Jose-Luis. I am not yet prepared to trust you and I have a family.'

He thought of Victoria and Eddie and the two girls, his nieces. Apart from Nancy they were undecided about him. He could tell. The years in the orphanage had taught him to read people. It would take time for Victoria to trust him, to realise that he wanted nothing except to be able to call her sister.

At that thought his heart swelled with joy. 'I have a sister. I am not alone. And I have my music and that will never desert me. If I live through this war I will finish my studies and then I will do what I can to repair all the damage.'

Life was good. Life was good.

'Here you are, Sandy, Officers' Mess. You can bunk with this lot. It's not the Ritz but the water's hot and the food's adequate. There are several other Scots here but, thank God, not all at the same time. Squadron Leader says you play the old Joanna a little. Maybe you can give us a bit of a sing-song after dinner.'

Xandro nodded as he opened the door and walked into the billet.

'Make the new boy welcome, lads. Name's Sandy Cameron, and he's from Glasgow.'

There were three men in the room and two of them, a young Pilot Officer and a slightly older Flying Officer, came forward to shake hands with the newcomer. The third was sound asleep on his bed and Xandro smiled as he recognised the shock of blond hair that would never do as it was told. He shook hands with the rest of the flight crew and then walked over to the bed.

'Don't wake him, Sandy. Great guy and superb pilot but he's grouchy as a bear with a sore head when he first wakes up. Our secret weapon, we call him. One of these days we're going to drop him over Berlin and let him snarl at old Hitler. That'll put a stop to this nonsense'

'I know he's grumpy,' whispered Xandro remembering years of shared dormitories and happy holidays.

He poked the recumbent figure, a Flight Lieutenant and therefore senior to all the men in the billet. 'Get up, you lazy trout. Is this the way the Royal Air Force greets new enlistments?'

Lazy eyes opened slowly and the others waited anxiously for the expected explosion. It did not come.

'Xandro? By all that's... How?'

He could not finish but jumped to his feet and hugged the slighter man.

'You never were able to take care of yourself, Jamie. I'm here to look after you. I'm your navigator. Alexander Cameron at your service, sir.'

Episode 11

There is always someone who profits from war. While most of the young men who had been to school with him were fighting and dying in all the theatres of the Second World War, Andrew Menmuir was making money.

After his release from prison he had, to all intents and purposes, vanished.

With no word from her son at all, Catriona invented scenarios of what might have happened to him. In her favourite one, he volunteered for the forces, was accepted despite his criminal record and was now redeeming himself *somewhere overseas*. One day soon there would be a letter or a telephone call. She just knew it.

Poor Catriona. Andrew had left prison

and taken the first train he could get back to Glasgow and to his underworld associates. By August of 1943 when Hamburg was almost destroyed by the combined weight of the Royal Air Force and its American allies, and the Honorable Jamie Fotheringham and his crew were involved in the successful bombing of a top-secret Nazi weapons base on Peenemunde Island, Andrew was running a night club in Liverpool and making so much money that there was talk of expansion.

Andrew loved money. He loved earning it, or rather, accumulating it, and he really liked spending it. In his club he patriotically framed a poster which showed two little men fashioned from reels of thread. One carried scissors in one hand and a knitting needle stuck through a fat ball of wool in the other.

Mend and make do, To save buying new, begged the poster.

Most people did – after all clothes rationing was said to have saved the country £600 million so far. But not Andrew. His double breasted suits sported large lapels; there were buttons on his cuffs and his trousers not only possessed lined pockets but they had turn ups. Thirty guineas changed hands

251

each time Andrew ordered a suit and no questions were asked about the twenty-six clothing coupons that should have been needed for the transaction.

While his brother-in-law was trying desperately to find anyone able bodied enough to help bring in the harvest which would help to feed the Nation, Andrew and his friends wanted for nothing.

Liquor and petrol were among the many hard to obtain items stored in Andrew's cellars. There were also crates of tinned goods. If anyone was going short it was not Andrew Menmuir.

Andrew sat at a table in *Andy's* and surveyed, with pride, the smoke filled noisy room. Loud laughter fought with the clarinet of the new jazz band he had hired to bring cosmopolitan culture to his patrons. He smiled with the pleasure of ownership, took a cigarette from the silver case he had ostentatiously removed from his breast pocket and offered the case to the young women sitting at the table with him.

'Go on, girls, plenty more where they came from.'

The girls smiled and took the cigarettes. Andy was fun. Being with him, it was easy to forget that there was a war on 'somewhere over there.' With Andy there was always music and dancing, lots of champagne, good food. He was always able to find nylon stockings, and lipsticks when all their chums were using beetroot juice, and petrol. He had a car, a sports car, and, when everybody was walking or cycling, 'doing their bit', it was joy to be taken for a spin with the top down. He was an absolute wizard with a machine, Andy was. Some of the girls had asked why he was not in the Army or better still, since he was so good with machines, why not the Air Force. With that dark hair and those blue eyes, he would look simply divine in the blue uniform, but better not to ask Andy questions. The blue eyes grew very cold. Much better to live for the moment.

'Jean, go on down the cellar and bring up some brandy for the Major. Got to keep our gallant soldiers up to par.'

Andy was at the bar with that crowd of arrogant young officers who spent more time there than they should. Jean, a waitress who was trying to earn a bit more to help out while the men of the family were overseas, shrugged her shoulders philosophically and went over to the door that led down to the cellars where Andy, *'his nibs'* had stores of everything.

She swore softly under her breath when the light on the stair failed to go on. Just like a man, plenty of cigarettes and wine, and the electricity needing a bit of new wiring. She was tired of telling him.

She got a candle from the emergency box behind the bar and with the limited light from it, made her way downstairs. There she searched among the boxes and cases looking for the bottles of brandy. He would want the best; that major was a favourite.

Jean put the candle down on an upturned box while she searched. At last; success. She took one bottle, picked up the candle, and headed for the stairs. Then she stopped. When had one bottle ever been enough? She returned to the cases, put her candle down and took out two more bottles. The candle, placed on an uneven surface, fell over and went out – or so Jean thought. Carrying her precious bottles she peered down at the dusty floor but saw nothing.

She shrugged again, kicked sawdust casually in the general direction of the candle, and returned to the stairs.

Three hours later, exhausted but, for once, perfectly content with the tips in her pocket, Jean went off home to her family, leaving her employer to close the club before going upstairs to his elegant flat.

An hour later the streets of Liverpool were rent by an explosion so fierce that people jumped from their beds fearing yet another air raid. But there had been no warning – no air raid warning – and yet the sky was bright with flames.

Another explosion blasted the ears of the startled people, and then another and then there was just the roar of flames.

The terrible news became wide spread.

'It's that fancy Night Club, it's gone up.'

'Jerry blow it up?'

'Never; they say that Scotch spiv had enough liquor and petrol down there to float a battle ship.'

It took several hours for the combined Civil Defence, police, and fire brigades to put the fire out. Two bodies were discovered and when they were able to be identified they proved to be the body of the owner, one Andrew Menmuir, and that of one Molly Armstrong, a young singer who had been a particular friend of Mr Menmuir.

Families have been notified, said the newspaper report.

If, in some parts of 'this green and pleasant land' the war was much in evidence, there were many places where it appeared, on the surface as if the war had passed it by. Crops were sown, they grew and were harvested. Cows were milked and sent out to graze, brought in and milked. But there were subtle changes that became less and less subtle. Able-bodied men went to war and land girls came in to take their places. Soon even the land girls, excellent as they had proved to be, were not sufficient for the work that had to be done. Families from the great overcrowded cities were invited to come to the country to help the great war effort by volunteering to bring in the harvest. Many did.

Flora Fotheringham allowed the gardens at Inchmarnock house to be dug up and vegetables planted. It was sad seeing the beds that had nurtured countless varieties of flowers go but Flora was philosophical. She had never lived as Lady Inchmarnock in this her husband's Scottish seat. As a giddy girl she had visited and had loved the house and the gardens but more, she had loved the son of the house, and for over twenty years, he had been her husband. Circumstance had sent them to Australia. Their son had never played on those great lawns, he had never run among the flower beds. Yet it was hard.

'Although they taste wonderful, vegetables are not usually so pretty as flowers.'

'Excuse me,' Connie, clicking away accurately on her typewriter, asked.

'I was thinking out loud, Connie dear. Saying vegetables aren't so pretty as flowers.'

'Depends on which flowers and which vegetables, Lady Inchmarnock,' said Connie deftly removing the typed sheet of paper and inserting another in its place. 'I think some flowers are perfectly hideous.' She thought for a minute. 'All the succulent ones. Give me a marigold any old day.'

'You are the strangest girl,' laughed Flora. 'What's our patient number?'

'Every bed full and everyone desperately seeking more – beds, not patients. We also need staff, Ma'am, everything from nurses to cleaners.'

Flora sighed. 'I suppose that was what your flying fingers were typing out now, Connie.' She laughed. 'Do you remember, my dear – is it even conceivable that two years ago you couldn't type at all?'

'Perseverance and patience. Your patience, my perseverance.'

'Well, I'll say it now in case I never find the

time again, but I couldn't possibly manage without you.'

In the dark days that followed that remark was put to the test more than once.

Would there ever be an end to the stream of recuperating servicemen and in some cases, injured miners from the Fife coal pits, who arrived at Inchmarnock house? Flora found fewer and fewer opportunities to return to Edinburgh to see her husband and she missed him. She sat at her desk and knew that just a few doors away was the lovely room where the family's greatest tragedy had occurred when Sandy's son from his first marriage, Robert, had committed suicide because of wounds suffered in that other 'war to end all wars.'

Since that day Sandy had not spent a single night under the roof where he had once been happiest. He was ill at ease when he visited her and Flora had decided never to let him see just how much she missed him. He had never really wanted her to go back to her early career and surely he would only say, 'Come back home if you miss me so much, old girl.' She could almost hear his voice and she smiled wryly. *Old girl.* How she would love to hear him call her that again.

She worked on for a few minutes and stopped. His voice. His beloved, well known voice; it seemed to be ringing in her ears. She put down her pen. It was his voice. She looked up as the door opened.

'Lord Inchmarnock, Ma'am.'

'Hello, old girl.'

Flora could say nothing. How very, very silly. Her heart was hammering as it hammered that first night when she had danced with him all those long, long years ago, the night she had fallen in love.

She struggled to her feet, her heart in her eyes. 'Oh, Sandy.'

'I'll check that requisition, Ma'am.' Flora barely heard the girl's voice as Connie slipped past Lord Inchmarnock.

When the door closed behind her Flora found her feet and was enfolded in her husband's arms.

She looked up into his beloved face. 'Sandy, why? There's nothing wrong is there?'

He kissed the tip of her nose before he released her. 'Yes, there is. I'm lonely without you and I thought – *all that's keeping you from your wife is your stupid attitude to the house.*'

'I understand, darling.'

'I know, always my most understanding patient wife, but when we came at the beginning of the war, Flora, you and Jamie and I, I didn't have nightmares about Robert. I can't forget he died here but I remember that he lived and played here too. He loved this house. I'll remember that.'

She looked at him in astonishment. Never would she have asked him to make such a sacrifice for her. 'You're going to stay?' she whispered, scarcely daring to hope.

With a wicked grin on his face he went to the door. 'I quite like the idea of making some lovely memories of our own here, old girl. I'll leave you to your work while I go and see if we can turn at least one of the lawns into silage. By the way, what a mess you've made of my mother's rose garden,' he finished with a grin as he went out, quickly shutting the door behind him.

Flora sat down at her desk and looked at the door. She heard his steps as he walked across the floor of the hall and she heard his voice as he met someone else, possibly one of their 'walking wounded'. A few minutes later she saw him walking past her window. He was pushing a patient in a wheelchair towards what had once been rose gardens and which were now destined to supply the hospital with cabbages.

'Corporal Trainer said, *Give us a shove into the garden, Mate,*' said Connie behind her. 'Has his Lordship ever been addressed as *mate* before?'

Flora laughed. 'Yes, and worse in Australia. Well, I think we've got ourselves a new porter, Connie. And we won't have to pay him.'

'Wonderful. Strike off the list one porter.'

'Porter, letter writer, reader,' said Flora and added under her breath, 'husband, lover, best friend.'

Professor Emil Piaseczany was determined to return to Poland to find his daughter. He went first to London where the Polish Prime Minister, General Sikorski, was living and where several senior Polish officials were anxious to help their fellow countrymen, if at all possible, but all the news that they brought Emil was bad. Mass graves of Polish officers found, Polish towns razed to the ground, Polish Jews disappearing. He was haunted by pictures that appeared in the newspapers of the Jews of Warsaw being systematically obliterated by the SS.

His Anneliese was alive, he knew it, he could feel it. She had not been exterminated. He had no idea where she was and he dared not think of what she was going through but she was not dead. He would know, surely he would feel it. Often he looked north towards Dundee and Angus and thought that perhaps he should have stayed there while his academic abilities could still have been of some use and where he had had the warmth of his friendship with Victoria to help him.

'Friendship, Emil,' he groaned. 'You love her almost as you once loved Eva. You are better alone in London.'

He went round and round the Resistance groups offering himself for any kind of work and at last he found himself in Gibraltar. He was not in Poland but he was nearer than he had been in London and with his facility in several European languages he was doing work of which he was proud.

'Please get me into Poland,' he begged, 'or even Russia. I can walk from there. I must find my little girl.'

From Gibraltar he wrote to Victoria.

I cannot tell you where I am or what I am doing but I am being useful. To feel oneself of use is very important. Of my daughter I hear nothing, Victoria, and sometimes the despair is so overwhelming that I wonder why I carry on.

It is, to all these officials with their lists, as if she never was. But she was and is. I know she is and one day I will find her and I will bring her to you and you will give her milk and eggs and she will grow well and strong.

And your little girl? She is growing more strong every day like your Nellie who lost her son. To lose a child, Victoria ... it is harder, my dear, than to lose a love.

Victoria did not know whether or not to agree with him. She had lost not one love but two.

For years she and Eddie had been growing farther and farther apart. Nancy's accident had brought them closer again as they comforted one another and their older daughter. Day after day they had sat by Nancy's bedside and had rejoiced as parents do as Nancy's health had improved. Then they had drifted apart again when Victoria had begun to see Emil. They no longer talked but as Victoria tried to analyse the situation she realised that they had not really talked to one another for years. They had been totally involved with the farm and their children: they had been the Welborns or the Farmers or the Parents but very very seldom had they been simply Eddie and Victoria.

263

'Perhaps we forgot how to be,' thought Victoria sadly as she packed her suitcases and arranged to move in with her mother.

She was not leaving Eddie, not as the world saw leaving one's husband. On her grandfather's death, all those years ago, Victoria had promised never to leave her mother. She had married, but only after Catriona had remarried a good man. She had stayed with Catriona after Davie Menmuir and his mother had died and now Catriona needed her again.

'Andrew's dead,' Catriona had said baldly on the telephone.

Victoria felt the room swim round her. What more? What now?

'How? When?' she managed to ask and Catriona, her voice full of tears had told her of the night club fire.

'I'll come,' Victoria said.

Catriona had tried to dissuade her. 'I'll be fine. It's a shock but by my age you have learned how to cope. I was so sure I was going to get a phone call, Victoria. I prayed he had changed, prayed he was doing good and now ... this. He's dead, my little boy and there was a girl with him, not his wife, but...' She stopped and Victoria waited. 'It's a re-lief in a way. I don't have to wait for the phone any more.'

'I'll come.'

Victoria put down the telephone and went into the scullery where Nellie Sinclair was scrubbing potatoes.

'Nellie, I'm going to stay with my mother for a few days. Will you help Eddie with Nancy?'

Nellie turned round and looked at her employer. She dried her red work worn hands on her pinnie. 'Are you all right, Victoria? Your eyes are like saucers stuck there on your face.'

Victoria gave a harsh laugh. 'Saucers on my face. Where do you get these sayings from, Nellie Bains?'

At the use of Nellie's maiden name both women laughed.

'We're getting past it if we're back tae Nellie Bains and Victoria Cameron,' said Nellie. 'Sit doon while I make you a cup of tea and tell me what's wrong, for something is.'

Victoria sat down heavily in a kitchen chair. 'Andrew has been killed in an accident. My mother needs me.'

Nellie gasped and then took a deep breath. 'It'll be a case of you needing each other. Poor Mistress Menmuir. She's had mair nor her share these past few years.'

Victoria looked at her and saw not only her old school friend but a woman whose only son had been killed in an air raid and who thought everyone else worse off than herself.

'Nellie Bains, has anybody told you how very special you are?'

'Ach away and stop blethering. There's nothing special aboot me. Life makes ye what you are, Victoria. You just have tae learn how to deal with it.' She handed Victoria a cup full of strong sweet tea. 'Here drink that up and then pack a few things. Nancy and Mr Menmuir'll be fine while you're away. You'll be going south, I suppose.'

Victoria drank deeply and tried to think. 'I have no idea. Mother just said she'd got word there had been a terrible accident. I suppose we'll arrange for him to be brought home.' Her hands began to shake and she put the cup down. 'What a damned mess this whole war is, Nellie.'

'Aye,' Nellie agreed shortly. 'Will you see Nancy afore you go?'

Wearily Victoria got up from the chair and very carefully put it back neatly under the table. 'I'll stop at the Long Meadow on my way. Thanks, Nellie.'

She went upstairs and stood in the bedroom she had shared with Eddie for over twenty years and knew that she was glad to have an excuse to go. She felt that she should grieve for her mother but she could feel nothing for her brother who had caused so much pain.

'And my marriage, and my worry over Emil? I'm numb. I can't really feel anything. If I knew that he was safe. It's over – before it really started, it's over. I'll stay with my mother through this and I'll have time to think. There's been so much going on and no time to think about it. My brother is dead.'

Victoria sat on the side of her bed, the bed she had shared with Eddie since the day they had come back to her beloved Priory Farm. Her brother was dead. But her brother was alive. Where was Xandro? He had visited and had then gone again. Nothing had been said about the farm but she had asked Mr Boatman.

'If he is legitimate, Victoria, then he inherits the farm under the terms of your grandfather's will. You and this young fellow are both legitimate children of John Cameron.'

'But I'm the elder, by nearly twenty years.'

The lawyer had looked down at her sadly. 'That signifies nothing in the eyes of the law of the land, Victoria. The male heir takes precedence. Mr ... what was his name? ... Alcantarilla-Medina, how outlandish. Since his parents were married he must be, in Scottish law, a Cameron and whatever he calls himself, he is the rightful owner of Priory Farm. I think we should negotiate. After all, you and Eddie have worked the farm for years ... possession etc etc. Don't worry too much.'

'In other words, let sleeping dogs lie.'

'A sensible attitude to canines, Victoria.'

If Xandro was a sleeping dog he was unaware of it. There was very little time to sleep. 1944 seemed to bring continuous sorties. The only points of joy on the daily or nightly compass were the camaraderie with the other air crews, and the flying meal. Jamie hardly knew which flying meal he enjoyed more, the one they were given before they left on a mission or the one that was ready for them, it seemed, the minute they returned, exhausted, often dispirited, sometimes euphoric if no pals had bought it.

Xandro had learned to tolerate great plates of bacon and egg swimming in grease. Jamie loved them and wolfed them down ravenously, as did the others while all Xandro could say was 'at least it's better than that awful salty porridge.'

A cup of decent coffee was all Xandro asked for in the morning and he promised himself that, when he was a world famous pianist, nothing but the smell of perfectly percolating coffee would disturb his morning. He got to like the smell of eggs and bacon. They meant that they were going out and better still they meant that they were safely home. The flying meal was a ritual all airmen liked.

Home? They all said, 'thank God to be home.' Yet, for Xandro where was home? An orphanage in Mexico, a dormitory at Fettes College, the Inchmarnocks, an iron bed in a billet with several other young men?

All of them, thought Xandro, and, at the same time, none of them, for home is definitely where the heart is. His heart was here with Jamie. In quiet moments when he lay trying to sleep, fearful, and at the same time, joyfully anticipating the call to action, he knew that he loved his friend, Jamie Fotheringham, oh, not in the way that one day he would love a girl like Connie, but differently. Perhaps it was what he would have felt for a brother, for was not Jamie the nearest to a brother he had ever had. Perhaps it was the kind of love he would one day feel for a child of his own, proud, protective, supporting, tolerant. He did not know but he acknowledged it and was happy. How awful to be in this world, especially in a time of war, and have no-one to love. The ultimate loneliness.

Jamie, on the other hand, who very rarely thought at all, and never about the workings of his heart, went to bed whenever he could and was instantly asleep. If he had been asked he would have acknowledged that he loved his parents and *oh, yes, probably old Xandro if we're really analysing,* and then he would have added a great list of girlfriends, the crew, friends, servants etc etc.

Neither was thinking of anything except the job in hand when they found themselves over France on a bombing mission. The crew was a mixture of commissioned and non-commissioned men with a sergeant pilot as the senior man and then Jamie, Pilot Officer the Honorable James Fotheringham. They were a team, a unit, and they almost breathed as one, four men from such widely divergent backgrounds who would probably never have met but for the war.

In less than two days the Americans had broken through the lines in Brittany. 2,000 allied bombers, Lancasters, Wellingtons, Thunderbolts, Mustangs and Lightnings and somewhere in the midst of it, Jamie and Xandro, had dropped 4,000 tons of bombs on enemy positions near the vital communications centre of St Lo.

Had they had time to think of anything other than the job they were doing Jamie and Xandro might well have wondered if there would be anything left below them at all after such a bombardment. And never, never think of lives lost, old, young, sick, well, bad, good. Concentrate on the job, keeping on course, automatic reaction to meticulous, thorough training.

Watch out for tracer bullets, dance for a split second in the search lights from below. In and out, fire, re-engage. Were the batteries from below weakening? Surely they could hold on no longer under such a terrible onslaught. The lights disappeared ... nothing, nothing, but the roar of engines on either side and the explosions from below. The lights streaked again skywards through the billowing clouds of smoke from the scenes of destruction below.

The noise was unbelievable but there were compensations. In the heat of action there was no time to worry about the appalling cold.

And then Xandro felt a searing pain and looked down with surprise to see blood bubbling from a wound in his thigh. At the same time the pilot's voice coughed, choked and was still.

'We're hit,' came Jamie's voice. 'Serge has bought it. You all right back there, Xandro, Paul?'

'No problems,' said Xandro and pulled off his scarf to staunch the blood.

'Good, we'll head back. Sandy,' he began and then laughed. The name still meant his father not his friend. 'Sandy, give me a course. Straight ahead for bacon and eggs will do.'

'What will the French give us? Certainly no salty porridge. It might be worth going down to get a decent cup of coffee.'

'After the war, dinner on me, boys, at the Folies Bergere. Even you, baby Paul.'

The gunner was scarcely nineteen years old, yet old before his time in experience but not of naughty French night clubs.

'Race you – after the war, sir,' said the boy

and then they were too busy trying to keep the damaged aircraft in the air to joke with one another.

'We're not going to make it,' said Jamie a few minutes later in just the same tone of voice as he had used all those years ago on the Rugby pitch. But he could no longer shout, 'pass it to me, you fool.'

The engines stuttered and spluttered, trying frantically to cough themselves into life, but it was no use. The damaged plane like some great injured swan attempted to bring itself to a safe landing but its wounds were too severe. As its life blood poured out, the plane dipped towards the ground and spiralled out of control, before slamming into the soft earth. For a moment there was silence and then with a great swoosh it burst into flame.

Episode 12

Victoria had planted a walnut tree in front of her house when she and Eddie were first married. She had planted it, with old Tam Menmuir's help, in well dug soil and apart from a little judicious pruning to ensure a nice shape had done very little to it. Year after year, once it started fruiting, it supplied the family with a splendid crop of walnuts.

'Dinnae plant it where the frost'll get it, no too much water, nor too dry, Victoria, and watch oot that ye dinnae gie it too much manure. That'll jist make for lush growth that any frost'll kill.' That had been Tam who could dig and talk at the same time.

Victoria remembered old Tam and her beloved grandfather every time she harvested the nuts. Each year she gathered some nuts for pickling and then waited until the rest began to fall naturally before gathering them for drying. It was part of her ritual.

She was sitting at the window of her old bedroom in her mother's house in Blackness Road when she remembered that she had completely forgotten the pickling. As Nellie's family had done without her shortbread the year that young Jamie had been killed, then this year Victoria's Christmas dinner would be without pickled walnuts.

It was as good a reason as any to go home. She had been with her mother now for two months and although she and Catriona had visited the farm every weekend or invited Eddie and Nancy to visit them in Dundee, there had been no real discussion between husband and wife.

Eddie had brought her the letter from Emil which had eventually arrived in Scotland and, painfully, she had pulled the door closed on that episode of her life. She did it regretfully and was ashamed of her regrets.

'But life's too short,' she argued with herself. 'I should have loved Emil: he needed me.'

But Eddie needed her too. And Nancy and Mary Flora. No, not Mary Flora. She had left college to work in a factory in England and she was loving it.

'Maybe I'll finish college, Mum, maybe not.' And then she had unconsciously echoed her mother's thoughts. 'Life's too short for worrying. I'm enjoying myself while I can and I'm doing something to help the war effort.'

Who was right and who was wrong? Was it wrong to fall out of love with one man? How had it happened? She had met a stranger who had brought a breath of sophisticated cosmopolitan air into her life and something in her had hungered for it. But she was married to a good man, a man she loved, the father of her children and the man who had taken her little farm and made it one of the finest in the area. She had no right to hurt him.

'I didn't mean to do it,' she excused herself and then remembered how often she had refused to take that as an excuse for any wrong doing from her children. How often one or other girl growing up had looked at her dolefully, surveying a broken glass or some spilled milk. *I didn't mean to do it.*

Broken glass and spilled milk were nothing compared with the breaking of marriage vows.

Eddie was somewhere in the fields when Victoria reached the house. Nellie was in the kitchen peeling potatoes and scrubbing vegetables.

'Hello,' she said casually. 'Mrs Menmuir able to cope, is she?' She had seen Victoria's suitcase.

Victoria sighed and sat down at the table. 'I think she has always been able to cope Nellie. Where's Nancy?'

'With Tam or her dad. She's aye with one or the other and will come to no harm. Put the kettle on and we'll have a cuppa. I'm

276

making soup and stovies for the dinner. You're staying then?'

Victoria got up and reached past Nellie's bulk for the kettle. 'I was worried about the walnuts.'

'Nancy and me pickled some for you,' said Nellie as if the harvesting of walnuts was a perfectly valid reason for a wife to suddenly return home to her family. 'She's grand if you just tell her what to do. Got everything stained brown, mind you, but what's a wee bit walnut juice when she's happy to be helping.' She emptied the dirty water down the sink and scraped the potato peelings together for the hens. *Waste not, want not.* 'She asks about the foreign laddie, him that was the piano player. I'm glad, Victoria, for she's stopped asking about my Jimmy and that makes life easier for me and Tam.'

'What does she ask?'

'Och, nothing much. When's he coming back. Did she tell him about her horse pictures, that kind of thing? He wrote to her a couple of times, and sent her some pictures of horses but we havenae heard from him in a while. There, that's the kettle ready.'

'I won't be a minute, Nellie. I need to see the walnut tree.'

Victoria left the kitchen with its lovely smells of simmering soup and went out into the garden. There was still Autumn colour and although Victoria loved the spring flowers, especially primroses, as she grew older she was tending to admire the bravery of autumn more and more.

She tidied a few leaves on the asters and chrysanthemums and removed one or two drooping heads and then, almost reluctantly, moved to stand under her walnut tree.

So many faces and voices came to her here but especially the voice of her grandfather.

A walnut shell day is when you are with the one you love most in all the world.

Her life had been blessed with many walnut shell days and for almost twenty-five years most of them had involved Eddie. There were few nuts left on the tree. She reached up and pulled down a large round green fruit, sniffed its strange almost citrus like perfume and put it into the pocket of her old burberry. Later she would prepare it and then when the shell was ready she would take her memories of Emil Piase-czany and close them inside. There would be dark days ahead when she would need them to brighten the sky.

The skies were dark over France. Smoke from burning buildings hung in the air or drifted for miles across devastated ports. The noise of screaming shells followed the smoke or raced it towards the sea but at last all was quiet while both sides licked their wounds and prepared to start all over again.

In the corner of a farm near the small town of St-Come-du-Mont, thick black smoke had been rising steadily from the remains of an aircraft. A farmer tending his pigs had seen the plane fall from the sky and when it had exploded into flame he had crossed himself, spat on the ground as if to clear his throat from the stench of hatred and death and carried on with his work.

'Of course I did not go,' he told his sister, Agnes when she questioned him, 'for nothing could have survived the fire.'

'God rest their souls,' she said.

He spat again. 'They might have been Germans.'

'They too have souls,' she said quietly and turned away to pray for the dead.

The Sergeant pilot was dead; he had died before the plane had spiralled into the earth. The boy gunner, who would now never have a chance to laugh and make merry with his comrades at the Folies Bergeres, was dead. If he had not been dead when the plane crashed he could not have survived the fire.

The Flying Officer had somehow been ejected from the plane as it fell and he lay, in a crumpled heap, some distance from the plane. Had anyone been watching from the thicket near the stone wall they would have seen him move and they would have heard him feebly groan.

He was alive and in some miraculous way, not seriously injured. As he had fought for his life he now fought for consciousness and at last he succeeded and slowly painfully pushed himself to his knees. He raised his head and through the blood that obscured most of the left side of his face he saw the remains of the bomber.

Fear and anger forced him to his feet. 'Xandro,' he whispered and staggered forward.

He went only a few feet before he fell again and just as he did so the last of the plane's fuel tanks exploded.

Jamie kept his face in the dirt while bits of the plane rained around him and tears coursed from his eyes and mingled with the blood and the dirt on his face.

'Xandro, my friend, my brother,' he

sobbed. 'I promised myself that I would always look after you.' He raised his face to the dark sky. 'Please, God, if there is a God, let him not have felt anything.'

'Actually, it hurts like hell,' said the somewhat shaky voice of Pilot Officer Sandy Cameron from behind him.

Jamie turned. Xandro was crawling painfully towards him from the thicket.

'Get away from that plane, idiota,' he yelled. 'I lost count of the explosions. There may still be more fuel or the odd bit of ammunition.'

Jamie pulled himself up and the two young men sat in the dirt and looked at one another and then they looked back at the plane.

'Serge bought it; oh, hell, Xandro, his wife is expecting their first baby. Why, why does it happen? He was such a damned good human being.'

Xandro said nothing for a while and still they sat in the dirt while their companions' bodies burned before their horror-stricken eyes.

'Any chance of getting anything personal ... for Paul's mum?...' Xandro didn't wait for the answer to his question; he already knew it. 'Pity we didn't get him to Paris. He loved it from the air.'

'We have to get out of here, Sandy. We're sitting beside a beacon that says, *Come and get us.*' But still they sat looking at the funeral pyre of their friends.

'You have to be dead,' said Jamie finally turning to Xandro.

'No,' said Xandro holding out his hands and staring at them as if somehow that proved he was alive. 'I fell out into that thicket; very thorny.' He smiled gamefully. 'Can you walk, amigo mio, because I don't think I can.'

Jamie saw that his right trouser leg was blood soaked and he stumbled to his feet and went to him. 'Xandro,' he could hardly go on and started to cry again.

'I took a bullet in the thigh and I've hurt something else, inside, I think. Everything hurts,' said Xandro. 'We had better get out of here. Jamie, if I don't make it ... you'll tell your parents how much they mean to me ... and you, of course. You have always been more of a brother than a friend. I suppose you British can't use the word love?'

Jamie made a sound not unlike a snort. 'Hardly cricket, old man, but ... ditto with me, Xandro, and you will make, damn it, if I have to swim the Channel pulling you

282

along behind me. Now enough of that soppy stuff. Jerry will check the plane, I think.'

He was not heavy: he had never been heavy, and Jamie almost welcomed his weight. God alone knew where they were and how badly Xandro was injured but they were alive. He hauled the slighter man up wincing as he heard Xandro's sudden intake of breath and held him as firmly but as gently as he could around the waist. Xandro managed to get one arm across Jamie's shoulders.

'I always hated rugby scrums,' he hissed through clenched teeth.

'Good practice for this, old chum. I'll try to find somewhere for us to hide until I've had a look at that leg and then we'll make some kind of plan.'

They stumbled on keeping to what little shelter they could find but Xandro seemed to grow heavier and heavier as he gradually lost consciousness. Then Jamie thought he heard a sound, perhaps someone approaching them through the bushes. He pulled Xandro against the remains of an old wall and lay down getting as close to his friend and the wall as possible.

Xandro moaned.

'Sh. Someone's coming; try not to make a sound.'

Obligingly Xandro lay slipping in and out of consciousness and Jamie peered into the gathering darkness.

A peasant woman, her shawl around her head and shoulders, was walking purposefully towards the field where the remains of their plane lay, still burning. Jamie held his breath. And Xandro moaned again.

The woman stopped, turned, and saw them. 'Mon Dieu, les pauvres,' she said.

Jamie had not done particularly well in French conversation at Fettes. In fact he had been particularly inept at foreign language, but he did gather from her tone that she felt sorry for them.

'Bonjour, Madame,' he said although it was growing dark. 'Comment allez-vous?'

There was a snort of laughter from the semi-conscious Xandro who pushed himself up and, to Jamie's astonishment, addressed the old woman in fluent French.

Jamie listened in astonishment. He supposed he remembered that Xandro had been good at French but no, he had always been the one in the background while he, Jamie, had made all the decisions. Still he looked on with pride as the old woman got to her knees beside them and gently examined Xandro's injured leg. She turned to Jamie and loosed a deluge of French around his head.

'Parlez-vous Anglais?' was all he could say in reply.

'Shut up, Jamie, your appalling French will get us shot. She's on our side. She wants you to help me to the farmhouse she shares with her brother.'

'Tres bien, Madame,' said Jamie and the old woman smiled at him and patted his head.

'See I do know some French,' said Jamie as he stood up and pulled Xandro up with him.

The short journey to the farmhouse was extremely difficult. Xandro, thankfully, was now completely unconscious, and he stayed like that during the journey and while the woman argued ferociously with her brother. He was coming round again as the old farmer, much against his better judgement, threw him over his shoulders like a sack of meal and carried him into the farmhouse's best bedroom.

Jamie helped the old woman, Agnes, to undress Xandro and wash his wounds. Without understanding a word of what he was being told he managed to carry out her orders and even held down the semi conscious Xandro while Agnes sewed up the great gash in his thigh. At last he was able to doze quietly in a chair beside the bed, a mug of some hot liquid, he thought it might once have been chocolate in his hand, while Xandro lay white and still under the starched cotton sheets.

For hours Xandro lay like one dead but later he began to move and to mutter deliriously.

Jamie woke completely and sat there talking quietly, occasionally holding the delirious young man down on the clean thin white cotton sheet. Mam'selle Agnes joined him for part of the night and Jamie thought once that his parents and Xandro would laugh at how her untried virtue would have been impossible to violate, even had he wanted to, by her armour of old coats.

'You'll be glad some day,' he told the old woman. 'Il sera one day tres famous. Il est un wonderful musician,' and she smiled at him, understanding not one word.

Most of that awful first night Jamie, beloved only son of Lord and Lady Inchmarnock and heir to title and great wealth, sat by the bed of his old schoolfriend and thought of how much Xandro meant to him and to his extended family. For half his life Xandro had been there, at first so small, so unassuming, until Jamie and his parents had realised that a heart of purest gold beat in the slight frame. An orphan, very possibly also an heir to money and power, he hated no-one and accepted his lot philosophically. According to him, God had given him one great talent, and he would work to be worthy of it. Jamie remembered him on the rugby field, 'bloodied but unbowed.' He remembered him sitting at the grand piano in the drawing room humbling them with his talent and he remembered him in the orphanage in Mexico, assuring the aristocratic old nun, Sister Mercedes, that he was true to his faith and to his talent, both gifts from God.

'Live Xandro,' he whispered. 'Don't die on me.' He remembered Xandro's halting words at the crash scene and how he, with his British stiff upper lip had glossed over the moment. 'I'm thinking, Xandro, me, old "live-for-the-moment." I adore my mother, and my old pa, they're total goodness, then there's you, and I remember all the times at school when you could have been wiped out but your courage and your

... what can I call it, quality, that's the word, that shone through, and I admired you. Now I admit that I love you and what's wrong with that, old friend. I'm a better person for knowing you, not because – if I can get home in one piece – you'll be a world famous pianist but because you're you, old thing. My friend who played tricks on me at school, who could take the home and livelihood away from friends of my mother if you chose and who won't, who plays silly little dance tunes on the piano for Constance when you'd rather be losing yourself in your beloved Beethoven. I'm thinking about Constance too, Xandro, and hoping I'll see her again.'

'Then shut up for a while and let me get some sleep,' said a tired pain filled voice. 'Otherwise, Jamie, my friend ... my brother, I'll find the strength to kill you myself.'

The news that the Honorable James Fotheringham had been shot down and was *missing, presumed dead,* travelled to Dundee in various ways. Catriona Menmuir read it in the Courier some days before Flora, Lady Inchmarnock, telephoned her.

She 'phoned Victoria.

'I just don't know what to do, Victoria.

288

Should I ring Dr Flora or should I try to write something?'

Victoria had seen the paper herself and had read that the entire crew of the bomber were *missing, presumed killed* and she was praying too for the repose of the soul of her half-brother, although the news item had not mentioned him by name.

'Mother, I'm very sad for the Inchmarnocks but did you remember that Xandro was flying with Jamie?'

'Xandro?' asked Catriona doubtfully and then she remembered. 'Oh, poor wee laddie,' she said. 'They say he would have been a great pianist one day.'

Victoria sat for a minute looking out of the window at the garden and the walnut tree. Beyond the garden, smoke was rising lazily from a fire that Tam was watching and she could see Nancy helping him to feed the fire and, at the same time, make sure that it did not spread. The autumn air brought the haunting smell of wood smoke to her through the open window. Somewhere in France, she wondered, had some other farmer's wife smelled the awful smell of the burning downed aircraft?

'I think it's better to write to Dr Flora, Mum. She'll be positive, you know. She'll refuse to believe he's dead, just as poor Nellie refused to believe, and they do say some boys turn up in prison camps who've been listed as missing. *Missing, presumed killed* means only that, as yet, they have found no bodies. Maybe some French people have found them and are hiding them. I think Lord Inchmarnock's the one who will be desolate and Dr Flora will be keeping his spirits up. After all, he's gone through this so tragically before with his first son, Robert.' She was quiet herself for a moment as she remembered Robert, her knight in shining armour, with his gentleness and physical beauty, so different from his half brother, Jamie. 'A letter from you will certainly help her.'

Catriona found the letter too difficult to write. She started several times but found that the words she wanted just would not come. Everything sounded banal or stilted.

Dear Dr Flora,

I was so sorry to hear of Jamie's...

And then Flora saved her by telephoning herself.

The phone call came one evening as Catriona sat going over the accounts from the garage.

'Oh, Dr Flora, I've been trying to find the

words,' began Catriona after she heard the loved voice.

'I know, Catriona, but there aren't any are there, old friend. I know what you feel and so does Sandy. He's in shock, of course, really looking his age, bless him, and that means, I have to suspect, that I'm beginning to look my age too but I won't give up, Catriona, until they show me my son's body. Time enough for mourning. It's more delicate than my Jamie, I'm afraid, Catriona. I wondered if you realised that John's son was in the plane with Jamie?'

John's son? Andrew was John's son and he had blown himself up. No, no, of course she meant the other boy, the Mexican.

Catriona wiped away a tear but who it was for she did not know and she did not question. Too many tears in too long a life.

'Victoria told me,' she said, 'but, oh, Dr Flora, I haven't got feelings for that boy. I'm sorry, of course, but there's been too much lately. Nothing's gone right since my dear Davie passed on.'

'Nonsense,' said Flora brusquely, in just the tone she had used all those years ago when she had been a young doctor battling disease and the odds in Dundee. 'We'll beat this, Catriona. We'll fight and we'll beat it just as we have always done. Nancy's much better. My Sandy is able to walk around his old home without seeing a sad ghost every time he enters what was his study. These are gifts and we must enjoy them. Now, you go and make yourself a nice cup of tea and I'll go and ring Victoria. She's probably wrapping herself up in guilt and grief too.'

'Guilt?' asked Catriona, fearing another shock.

'If our lovely Xandro is dead then he cannot possibly take her farm away from her and she's bound to feel relieved about that and, at the same time, she was beginning to love him – he is her brother, after all – and she's upset that she's lost him before she even really knew him.'

That was too complicated for Catriona. How could one feel guilt and grief over a death unless one had somehow, even unwittingly, caused the death? She went back to her account books. Figures caused her no problems. They were either right or wrong.

Nancy opened the piano at her granny's house and started to delicately strike the keys. The noise, for it was not music, was not unpleasant. Only Xandro had played the piano since Davie's death and Eddie got up to distract his daughter's attention.

Catriona stopped him. 'She's not doing any harm, Eddie. If she starts thumping it like a baby we'll stop her, but you're not going to do that to Granny, are you, pet?'

'Where's Xandro?' asked Nancy and her three elders looked at her.

'She never once asks about her sister,' began Victoria.

'Mary Flora's in England,' said Nancy again surprising her parents and her grandmother with her returning abilities. 'Where's Xandro?'

'We don't know, dear,' said Catriona.

'He's dead, like Jamie,' sobbed Nancy and banged the piano lid shut.

She did not want her parents or her grandmother to comfort her but asked desperately for Nellie and it was some time before Victoria and her mother could sit down together and talk.

'We're off to feed the ducks,' said Eddie a paper bag of old bread in his hand he shepherded Nancy to the front door.

Victoria watched them walk off down Blackness Road. From the back Nancy looked like a slim young woman but the hat on her head was a child's hat and the mittens on her fingers, a child's mittens. Was her injury and illness a judgement on her friendship with Emil? No and again no. God would not punish a child for the sins of her mother. Victoria sighed and turned away from the window.

'The piano must have reminded her of Xandro,' said Catriona as she turned her chair into the warmth from the fire.

Victoria sat down near her mother and held out her hands for the wool Catriona was winding into balls.

'I think I'll knit a jumper for Jamie Fotheringham,' she said with an attempt at brightness.

Victoria said nothing but merely waited patiently, her arms outstretched.

'Did Doctor Flora speak to you, dear?'

'It all came back, you know, Mother, Robert's death. Poor Lord Inchmarnock. The Great War killed his first son and this damned one has taken his second. Dr. Flora won't accept that he's dead and I don't know whether that's for her sake or for his lordship's.'

Catriona finished winding the light blue wool. 'This was a sweater I began years ago for Andrew,' she said. 'It'll look good on Jamie.' She began to cast on her stitches and Victoria watched her, mesmerised. She had never herself mastered the art of knitting and yet her mother and her second mother-in-law, old Bessie Menmuir, had both been excellent needlewomen who had tried hard to instruct her. 'I sometimes thought Dr Flora had a direct line to the Almighty, Victoria, but it's not that. She refuses to believe that her son is dead because no one has proved that he is. I pray for all their sakes that she is right but I find it hard to believe that anyone could survive being shot down and other members of the Squadron saw them being hit and saw them going down. Xandro Alcantarilla or Sandy Cameron, as he was calling himself, was on the plane too and the Inchmarnocks are distressed about him too. He was a part of their family.'

'He was my brother,' said Victoria, 'and for months I have had the most ambivalent feelings about him. He was so young, so talented, so kind but, at the same time he reminded me of my father – the eyes, I think, beautiful eyes. And then, since he was ... legitimate, he has a right to Grandpa's farm, the farm Eddie slaved over, and I worried about that. Now it looks as if all my worries were for nothing because if he's dead, he can't challenge us for ownership, and quite frankly, I would rather he was here, alive, playing Davie's piano.'

'Did he want the farm?'

'Dr Flora said he wanted only to be part of the family, that he was perfectly content with his music studies, but I didn't make him welcome.'

Catriona looked at her daughter. Poor Victoria. She was so hard on herself and Life dealt enough blows on its own without embracing more.

'The only time he was ever at the farm you gave him a good meal, lassie, and showed him round.'

'I could have done more. Even when he wrote to Nancy, it was Eddie helped her answer them. Well, if Lady Inchmarnock is refusing to admit the laddies are dead, maybe I'll refuse too and when they are rescued I'll tell Xandro or, Sandy is it, to come home to Priory Farm.'

Anneliese Piaseczany had walked for hours, days, weeks; she could no longer remember. With Vilem's help, she had managed to find some potatoes half frozen in a field and she had eaten them. They had drunk the water from a puddle, muddy and oil streaked but they had laughed cracked distorted laughter as they had compared it to the water they had been drinking in the camps. They had no idea where they were, even in which country they found themselves. They had been together, two Polish Jews, since the Pogroms in Warsaw. They had been herded from one camp to another at the whim of some deity they never saw and no longer even thought about. Life was work and hunger and pain and fear until Vilem had lowered her over the tailgate of the lorry as it had slowed down on the dark road. He had, of course, jumped after her, for without him she would simply have lain down in the road to die.

Now their life was hunger, pain, and fear unless the effort of keeping alive and moving was work in which case nothing much had changed.

But no, Anneliese thought suddenly and the thought was like a skylark erupting into a blue summer sky, everything was changed because they were free. The sun had gone down twice or maybe it was three times. When you are starving it is difficult to keep track of time. No matter, in two or maybe three days no one had screamed at them, no one had struck them and no bullets had come racing through the air towards their defenceless, filthy, young bodies. Maybe the guards had not counted or perhaps they did not care whether they delivered five or fifty Jews to the new concentration camp.

'There is a light up there, Anneliese,' whispered Vilem. 'We must find food. You lie here in the ditch and I will go forward and listen. If I hear German I will creep back.'

She clung to his hand. 'No, Vilem. We go together.'

She could not go on alone without him. All her short life she had depended on her beloved father and then when Papa went to Scotland and the unthinkable had happened, Vilem had been there.

'If we're in Poland, Anneliese, you can go on if anything happens to me. God did not help us only to turn His back now. I know this. You wait here and I will come back to tell you,' but still she refused to let him go.

Thinner than two sewer rats and twice as dirty the youngsters crept forward. Ahead of them there rose the dark shape of a small farmhouse. A chink of light showed at a window. Someone was there. Forward they went again and then they heard a sound that they had learned to fear and hate, the deep throated growling of a dog.

Anneliese turned to stone where she lay in

the dirt. She could not move, no matter the provocation. She could not even pray that the dog was tied up. Once she had seen a man killed by prison dogs. Any death was preferable but still she could do nothing to prevent it. Vilem lay beside her, his thin young arm protectively over her head.

The dog was barking now and they could hear his chain as he pulled and pulled in his frantic wish to find them and tear them to pieces.

'Shut up, Boris.' The man stood at the door, light spilling on to the ground before the cottage. 'What have you found, old man?'

The language was German. Vilem pulled himself up and carried Anneliese with him. If they were to die they would face it, not lie in the dirt waiting for it.

'Mein Gott, what have we here?' The man, the dog and the two youngsters looked at one another. They saw an elderly man, obviously a farmer, and he saw two scarecrows with the tattoos of their prisons etched into the skin of their painfully thin arms.

He smiled but it was not the smile of evil intent or enjoyment that they had experienced so often. It was a smile of goodness.

'Ach,' he said slowly. 'Poor, poor children.

God is good. You will be safe here.'

He picked up Anneliese as if she was a doll and walked towards the open door with her while Vilem stood, still petrified, and watched.

The man stopped, his burden as nothing in his strong farmer's arms. He turned his head. 'Come boy, not all Germans are fiends. There is not much inside; soup and bread and maybe a bath, and then sleep. I will watch through the night, me and Boris, and no-one,' he said, his old eyes twinkling, 'no-one gets past Boris.'

Vilem smiled shakily and then staggered after him into the cottage.

Episode 13

The Honorable Constance had become the ideal secretary. She knew everything and could do anything, quickly, efficiently. Her immediate superior, Flora, Lady Inchmarnock, thought her quite indispensable. Even though she herself found it difficult to keep up a front of cheer and belief and was sometimes, in the privacy of her office, so overwhelmed with grief and terror that she felt her body must shout its pain through the whole house, she was professional enough to realise that Connie too was suffering. They had celebrated Christmas of 1944 and New Year of 1945 with as much cheer as they could manufacture – there were seriously wounded young men in the great house – but there was no heart in Connie's carols, no real joy as she kissed the walking wounded below the mistletoe that Lord Inchmarnock had gathered from the trees around his Scottish seat, this great house that had become a hospital.

'God wouldn't do it to him twice.'

That was Flora's belief and she knew that there was absolutely no reasoning behind it. Many people lost their sons, just look at that poor family in America, the Sullivans. Seven sons, was it, that they had lost. Did they blame God or did they blame man who was given free will, perhaps the most generous of the abused gifts?

It became her mantra – God wouldn't do it to him twice.

She repeated it to Connie.

'Oh Ma'am, you know that's nonsense, this has nothing to do with God.'

Flora reached over and grabbed the girl's

shoulders. She looked into the young face, a face that was pale and strained and had dark shadows under the eyes. 'Saying it makes me feel better, Connie. Tell me, child, is it me you weep for, or my husband, or is it for yourself?'

Connie looked at her. What could she say? What was the right thing? The truth is best, always the truth. 'All of us, Lady Flora. I really didn't know how much he meant to me but since he left, I keep remembering silly things, his making Xandro play schmaltzy songs or Christmas carols, his truly appalling sense of humour, his gentleness, oh, in a minute you'll have me thinking I might be in love with him.'

Flora reached for the telephone which had just started to ring. 'Lady Inchmarnock,' she said into the receiver, 'Please hold for a moment. Connie, could you say all those things to his father, get him to talk, please, my dear. He needs to talk. You'll know how to start.' Then again she was the efficient doctor, the Director of a hospital with no time to think about the fact that her only child was missing in action.

Connie went out onto the terrace and stood for a moment looking over the gardens. Winter was over and the spring flowers were everywhere in evidence in the wild parts of the estate but here the gardeners, mainly walking wounded, were busy planting next summer's vegetables in what had once been glorious rose gardens. A tall slender man, in a disreputable old tweed jacket and a hat that should by rights have gone to any of the poor desperate enough to take it, years ago, was weeding conscientiously.

Connie walked down the path. 'Lord Inchmarnock.'

He straightened up and with old world gallantry removed his hat. 'Hello my dear. Am I being summoned?'

She looked into his kind eyes. 'No, sir. I need your help. You see, I find I miss Jamie more than I ever thought I would and, oh forgive me if I'm wrong, but I thought it might help if we talked.'

He looked at her for a moment and she thought she had gone too far. Jamie was his son, his only child.

He smiled at her, Jamie's smile. 'Do you know, Connie, my dear, he never played in these gardens as his brother did but, strange thing is, I keep seeing him here. I hear him laughing and I think...' He tucked her arm into his and started off down the path towards the duck pond. 'Sometimes I think I'm mixing them up, my darling boys. They didn't look at all alike, you know. Robert was physically very ... silly word, but beautiful, I suppose, and Jamie was, IS, Jamie is Jamie. Did I ever tell you about the year he met Xandro?...'

From her window Lady Inchmarnock watched them walking down the garden paths, arm in arm, heads close together, laughing heartily, crying maybe.

'God wouldn't do it to him twice,' she said again and went back to the lists of boys for whom she somehow had to find a bed and medical attention.

'Anneliese, my darling child, how are you ever going to make a man a good wife if you can't even milk a cow or pluck a chicken?'

Anneliese smiled up at Dieter Kraus. Her fear of this large German was gone. He was not at all like any other German she had ever met. In fact, he reminded her of her gentle, sophisticated father. He loved music and whistled operatic arias all day and, she had not the heart to tell him, he was always off-key, but he recited poetry to them in the evenings, Goethe, of course, but Shakespeare too and even Lord Byron. For the first few weeks that they had been with him she and Vilem had lain quietly in two little handmade wooden beds on scrupulously clean white sheets and he had washed them and fed them and sang his excruciating operas and they had begun slowly to get well, to stop freezing at the slightest sound, to eat the simple food that he prepared for them without falling on it like starving dogs, to go outside in the good clean air like normal people, to sleep – sometimes without dreaming.

Anneliese had grown strong more quickly than Vilem, for he had sacrificed so much for her had shared what little food he could scrounge with her, and therefore he was so much weaker. She had not known Vilem in her village; she had met him in one of the camps but she could no longer remember when or in what camp. She loved him as she had loved her papa and she would never be parted from him again and she knew that he loved her although he had said nothing, stolen no kisses as Ivan had done, oh so long ago.

She hitched up the sleeves of her shirt, a shirt that Dieter's son had worn years ago before he had gone, like too many German boys, to die in a war they did not believe in, closed her eyes and started again on the old hen.

Dieter watched for a minute and then took the hen away. 'There is nothing for it, liebling, we will have to find you a rich husband. Go inside and turn on the wireless and see what news there is today.'

Thankfully Anneliese left him with the tasks that still had to be done and returned to the tiny cottage.

Vilem was standing in the middle of the kitchen floor, the firewood he had just chopped still held in his arms.

'Vilem,' began Anneliese but he put out his hand to stop her talking and, in doing so, dropped the wood. It lay on the floor between them and Anneliese looked at it as she became aware that the old wireless was on and that Vilem was listening intently.

She too stood, ignoring the wood, and listened.

'What does it mean?' she whispered when the broadcast ended and Vilem switched it off before the start of the martial music that the local station played. He could not bear martial music.

He bent down and began to pick up the wood. 'I don't know. The end, I think, I pray.'

'Let's tell Dieter; he's given up trying to teach me to be a farmer.'

A look of horror crossed Dieter's thin face. 'We can't tell him, we can't. He's lost, Anneliese, his side has lost.'

She went to him and put her thin young arms around his frail body. 'Vilem, he lost all that matters to him years ago. You must stop thinking of him as German. He's just a man, Vilem, just a man, a good man.'

He said nothing and she held him until the shaking stopped. Oh, his body was healing, but his mind ... how long, if ever, would it be before it healed. Vilem, unlike Anneliese did not have the memories of a loving family to hold on to.

She took his hand. 'Come, my love,' she said gently, 'we will tell him that soon it will be over.'

He went with her to the dilapidated old barn where Dieter had just finished plucking the last of his old hens. He looked up and smiled as he saw them.

'Ach, you are a nice German story, hand in hand, the babes in the wood,' he said. 'Look, we will have chicken soup tonight.'

'Hitler is dead, Dieter.' There was no other way to say it.

He looked at them in stunned disbelief

and then he fell to his knees and began to cry. 'God rest his soul,' he said, 'and the souls of all he caused to die.'

Later that night he sat quietly in the cottage while the two youngsters lay sleeping and planned and schemed and worried. A dying dog is always more dangerous than a young healthy animal. He would have to be very careful of his two children. For months now he had kept them hidden, mainly because his farm was so isolated and because his neighbours had feared the anger, after the death of his son, which had caused him to hit out at everything. But now, good and bad together would be on the move, looking for a place to hide. He would guard them with his life, his little Anneliese and poor, scarred Vilem. His own boy would have been about the same age, maybe a year or two older.

Anneliese's father? The Professor. Professors were important, respected. Maybe now he could get a letter to him. Where was it she thought he was? A university somewhere. He would not wake her up. He found a few sheets of writing paper in the kitchen drawer. Dundee, that was it. Dundee in Scotland. Beethoven wrote about Scotland and Mendelssohn, maybe he would go there and deliver his children to the Professor. Even a clever professor would have to be told how to deal gently and delicately with the injured Vilem.

He thought carefully, drew the paper towards him, licked the stub of the only pencil he could find and began to write.

Esteemed Professor Piaseczany,

For several months now a delightful young lady has done me the great honour of taking shelter in my poor home. She is accompanied by a boy called Vilem who is, I believe, Czecho-slovakian. It appears that Anneliese met him in some ghastly camp. The boy helped her to escape and, if what she says is true, and I see no need to doubt her, he has kept her alive at times when her spirit sought to die. They have stayed safely hidden here on my farm but today I hear that Hitler has committed suicide and I worry about the flood of refugees who will possibly pass my land on their way – somewhere, anywhere but away from retribution. I am, as you can see from the heading, very close to the border with Poland. The Russians, I think, are now in Poland and so the children should be safe there. I could try to smuggle them across the border. On the other hand, perhaps I should try to get them to Britain. It is now mid-April and if I do not hear from you before the middle of June, I

will try to get them safely to Scotland.
  Your obedient servant,
  Dieter Kraus.
Eventually Dieter's letter reached the university offices and was passed around departments until someone who had met the Polish professor at a faculty meeting found it in his in-tray.

'Didn't Emil Piaseczany go back to Poland to try to find his daughter?' he asked.

Two weeks after the letter arrived in Dundee a secretary heard about it and remembered that she had heard that the Professor had gone to London, to the Polish Embassy.

The Embassy confirmed that Professor Piaseczany had been working in Gibraltar and gave a safe address there to which the letter might be redirected.

Mrs Archibald in the office redirected the letter and put it, still with its German stamp, in her out tray.

It was June 11th 1945.

Mussolini killed by partisans, Hitler dead at his own hands. Germany capitulated on May 7th. Three power occupation of Germany took place and Churchill, Truman and Stalin met at Potsdam. In Britain there

310

was a Labour landslide in the General Election but in the Far East the war went on.

Young Flora Sinclair wrote a letter from Edinburgh where she had been, first studying and later working, to her mother's employer, Victoria Welborn. To Victoria's surprise Flora asked if they might meet, in secret, in Dundee.

Victoria was at the restaurant early and booked a table in a quieter part of the main room. She wondered idly what the great secrecy was about. It had been some time since Flora had been home, since she had graduated from Teachers' training college and had managed to get a nice job teaching Primary 3.

'She loves it,' said the proud mother. 'Mind you Tam and I wish she'd tried for a local job so she could bide at home but young ones nowadays, they can hardly wait to get away. Look at your own Mary Flora.'

'At least,' thought Victoria as she waited, 'Nellie's Flora had finished college unlike our daughter.'

Nellie and Tom had been beside themselves with happiness the day of that graduation even though austerity meant there wasn't such a grand celebration as when

Jimmy had graduated. They had even managed to mention Jimmy at the party without crying and spoiling Flora's day.

Where on earth was she? Victoria hated waiting. There was always so much to do and to sit twiddling her thumbs in a restaurant was not her idea of time well spent.

'Sorry, Mrs Welborn. The bus was a wee bit late.'

Victoria looked up and saw a young Nellie but a sophisticated, educated, well dressed Nellie.

'Flora, my dear, you look so lovely and just like your mother.'

Flora smiled as she sat down. 'Thank you. That's a real compliment. My dad always says she was the bonniest lassie he'd ever seen.'

Victoria signed for a waitress to come to the table since it was obvious that whatever Flora wanted to say, she was having difficulty getting it out.

They chatted inconsequentially while the waitress brought tea and scones and rich cakes and then while Victoria was pouring hot water into the silver tea-pot, Flora blurted out, 'I'm going to have a baby.'

Victoria almost dropped the pot but she finished pouring while her brain worked furiously. What on earth was she to say? So many questions but where to start?

'Your mother doesn't know?'

Tears welled up and spilled over and Flora tried to wipe them away. Her handkerchief was already wet and so Victoria handed her a clean one.

'Why not, Flora? She'll have to know.'

'She'll think I've disgraced her.'

Victoria thought of Nellie who had cheerfully sat in the very same restaurant with her over twenty years before with her runny-nosed fatherless toddler. Nellie would not even think the word 'disgrace.'

'You're wrong, dear, not Nellie.'

'It's not that, Mrs Welborn and I'm not ashamed,' Flora said and lifted her head managing to look proud and scared at the same time. 'Peter loves me, or at least he did but there's losing Jimmy and me being a teacher and them being so proud of me. Oh, it's such a mess. I worked so hard to try to make up for Jimmy being killed and now I've ruined it all.'

Tread warily, tread warily. What would Nellie and Tam think if they heard their daughter. They had been so proud of their son, what parent would not be proud of a boy like Jimmy, but surely Flora was not second best. They themselves missed Mary Flora but at least she had never been made to feel that she had to 'make up' for wee Nancy. She was following the beat of her own drum and that meant interrupting her education to do war work. What she would do now that the war was as good as over Victoria did not know. But that was up to her.

'Flora, you have to tell your parents; they'll support you through this.' She could not say, 'they were in your place once'. That was for them to say.

She offered the girl the cake plate but Flora shook her head; watching her figure, no doubt, thought Victoria, the mother. She chose a plain sponge cake and cut it very carefully into small pieces while she worked out what to say.

'Flora, may I ask about ... Peter, you said?'

'He's dead,' said the girl dully and her heart was in her sad eyes. 'He was called up, you see, and when I knew he was going over seas, well, I hoped, I prayed he would come back. We had a weekend, one weekend at Portobello. It was the most beautiful two days of my entire life.'

'I'm glad you had that, dear, glad that the two of you had that. What do you want me

314

to do, Flora? Your mother's heart is as big as the ocean and your dad's quiet, especially around Nellie, but he's one of the finest men I've ever had the honour to know. They'll be pleased, once they're over the ... well, the initial surprise.' She could not ask how Peter had died, or where, or how Flora knew. These were questions for Nellie and Tam.

'Peter's family?'

'I don't know. We only talked about each other; there was never any time.'

No, there was never time. The older she got, the more Victoria realised that she had to make time, time to tell Edward that she loved him, time to tell Catriona that she had been a wonderful mother, time to tell Nellie that more than once the mistress had learned from the maid.

'When's the baby due, Flora?'

'The end of August.'

Victoria reached out and grasped the hands on the table in front of her. 'Wonderful,' she said. 'That is quite wonderful. We'll have a party at the Priory to welcome him. This awful war will be over. What a precious harvest he'll be, Flora, the most precious gift of all. Come on, lass. I'll drive you home and you tell your parents the good news, the wonderful news, a new baby at Priory Farm, a wonderful new beginning.'

Slowly Sandy Cameron got well. As Jamie said, he recovered in spite of Mam'selle's nursing, but that was unfair as Mam'selle was devoted to her young patient and although she had no medical degree, she had learned a great deal from the folklore of her family.

There was something wrong inside the boy. Ergo, he was to remain flat and they would pray to Le Bon Dieu that he would recover. In the meantime while they prayed, there were herbs to be gathered from the countryside, herbs that had helped count-less people before now. Since it was im-possible to find a doctor, 'Le Medecin, Madame?' screeched Jamie, desperately culling up words from Lower Fifth French, Jamie allowed the administration of potions and watched the gentle application of salves but he never left the bedside until once he woke to find himself undressed and in a bed of his own. Terrified he rushed to Xandro's room and found him lying quietly, talking in his excellent French to their elderly host.

'Hello, Jamie. I'm glad you fell asleep; Yves was about to hit you over the head to force you to get some rest.'

'Yves?' asked Jamie dully.

'Our host,' said Xandro, 'and you must be nice to him because he really doesn't want us here. He's terrified of being called either a collaborator or a traitor. Poor old thing is just afraid of everything except his pigs.' He was smiling furiously at the saturnine old farmer who sat whittling a stick at the end of the bed. 'Mam'selle, his sister, has gone to market but really she wants to hear if anyone has been looking for bodies in the wreck. Smile nicely, Jamie, I've told him you're a milord and he doesn't want to be impressed but he is.'

Jamie smiled nicely and the toothless old man smiled back and bowed low.

'They've been wonderfully good to you, Xandro,' said Jamie bowing again like someone in a music hall farce. 'But tell me, where on earth did you learn to speak such good French. You didn't take it at Fettes, did you?'

'Yes, I did, for my last three years, but it was Mother Mercedes who was my first and best teacher. You are so ignorant of anything outside Scotland, Australia and rugby, Jamie Fotheringham. Mexico had French as a second language, not English. We Mexi-

317

cans found you British so barbaric.'

'I'd show you barbaric, you cheeky blighter, if you didn't have something wrong with your tum. Feeling better? You look a bit brighter.'

'I could sit up, but Mam'selle is worried about my insides and it's quite nice just lying here being spoiled. The war seems so far away as I lie still and Yves whittles. We'll see what Mam'selle has to tell us and then, as soon as I can move, we must go. Yves,' he said smiling at his host, 'Yves says there are fishing boats not too far away. We're in Brittany and not too far from the coast, but we have to know where German patrols are.'

'No maquis or resistance around?'

It was obvious that the old man recognised these words even with Jamie's execrable pronunciation.

Xandro spoke to him quietly and seriously and then turned to Jamie. 'What did you do in French class at school, Jamie? There were actually one or two not bad teachers, but the thing is, we're on our own. We'll make for the coast and you will have to keep your mouth shut. I, for once, mon ami, will do all the talking, and I hope we meet no-one until we get to this little harbour Yves has been telling me about. Their cousin Jacques' brother-in-law, Oscar, has been known to make little visits to the south of England.'

'Good lord, smugglers. What will my papa say?'

Xandro smiled but the eyes were tired and Jamie watched as the long dark lashes fluttered and then lay still on the pale cheeks. He had been so close to death that Jamie still worried. He checked Xandro's pulse and the slow rise and fall of his chest. Everything seemed all right. Old Yves laughed at him, his rheumy old eyes saying that he knew perfectly well that Jamie thought Mam'selle and her salves and herbal remedies not good enough. He said something but Jamie could not translate the words that said that their medicines had been successful for hundreds of years.

Jamie gestured and tried to find the French for 'I will sit with him now, thank you.' Yves understood and soon Jamie saw him walking across the field outside the window towards the tin hut where his beloved pigs wallowed blissfully.

Jamie continued to sit while Xandro slept and, at last, he saw Mam'selle peddling her old bike along the road from the town. He went outside to carry her parcel for her and to prop the bicycle up against the old barn and when he returned she was in his chair in the bedroom and Xandro, a spot of feverish colour on each cheek, was talking in suppressed excitement.

'No-one has even bothered to look at the crash site. Can you believe it; two men dead, four for all they knew, and no-one has even bothered to look. Monsieur L'Abbe, the priest, is going out to retrieve the bodies – if there's anything left, and Mam'selle will keep the tags and watches, whatever. If it's done before we leave, we'll take them with us, otherwise she'll send things when it's safe.'

'Vous etes tres gentille, Mam'selle,' tried Jamie and wished he hadn't because she immediately fired a volley of French at him, most of which went right over his head.

'Never mind, Jamie,' laughed Xandro. 'By the time she allows me out of bed, you'll have learned a lot more than *ou est la plume de ma tante*.'

Puebla, Mexico

Mexico had declared war on the Axis powers in 1942. At first her contribution to the war effort was to refuse access to her ports to German or Italian ships but in

1944 Mexico sent a squadron of fighters to join the Allied Air Forces. Their theatre of operation was the Philippines.

Mother Mercedes was very proud. Her old hands toyed with the cover of the album in which she kept the life history of Alejandro Alcantarilla-Medina as she sat in the late summer sun and reflected on the progress of the war. Xandro had not written to her in some time and she knew what that meant. Had he been able, he would have written to her. If possible, during the last two years when, naughty boy, he had given up his studies to join the British Air Force she had prayed more than ever. Laborare est orare. To work is to pray but while she worked, such work as they would permit an old woman to do these days, she had also prayed in her head and her heart.

Lately the prayers were merely, *Blessed Mother of God, I trust you. Thy son's will be done.* What more was there to say?

There was a tap at the door and Sister Marie Estaban stood there, a thin piece of flimsy greyish paper in her hand.

'They said you were sleeping, Madre,' she said, 'But I knew you would want this immediately.'

Mother Mercedes held out a frail hand

which she would not allow to shake. 'Gloria in Excelsis Deo,' she said.

'Not one person has refused us, Nellie,' said Victoria happily, as she transferred yet another tray of scones from the oven to the scrubbed table in the kitchen. 'Mum's bringing some tins of ham – we won't ask where she got them – and she's made the Christening Cake. She's surpassed herself, if I'm allowed to say so.'

'You've been great to my lassie, Victoria,' said Nellie and Victoria looked at her housekeeper and former school friend and saw that there were tears in her eyes.

'Nellie Bains, not another word, and take that pot off the fire before you burn it.'

'You and your Nellie Bains,' said Nellie but she laughed which is what Victoria had intended.

'Heavens, what a party we'll have. My Mary Flora's twenty-first was the last thing we had to celebrate and what a lot has happened since then.'

They were silent for a while as they worked, their hearts full of the knowledge of deaths, and illnesses, and losses, and unremitting sacrifice and love of the past five years.

'It's all life, isn't it, Victoria?' said Nellie who had moved on to buttering scones. 'Are their lordships coming? I'll need to wear Jimmy's graduation dress if they're coming.'

Victoria wanted to but did not laugh. The dress Nellie had worn when her beloved son had graduated was only worn on occasions of the greatest solemnity now and then only for a few minutes for the speeches and then an old dress put on that Nellie could work in but if their lordships – Nellie's way of talking about Lord and Lady Inchmarnock – were coming, then THE dress would be worn for the entire party.

'I don't know, Nellie: I wish I could tell you. My mother always thought it was his Lordship would break down, after losing his first son in the Great War, but he's been strong; it's only been work that has kept Dr Flora from giving in to despair. Now with the war as good as over and fewer boys coming to the hospital, she has time to think.'

The telephone rang and Victoria wiped her hands and went to answer it. She came back to the kitchen looking quite annoyed.

'That's the third time this week. That dratted thing rings, I say hello, and all I hear is ... I don't know ... air, I think.'

'Wouldn't have one of them machines if you paid me,' said Nellie. 'More nuisance than anything. What were we saying, oh yes, Tam and me was hoping they'd be God-parents seeing as how Flora was named after her ladyship and their wedding and Flora's birth were at the same time.'

'What a lovely idea. Has Flora asked them?'

'She didn't like. It's him not having a father as they say and them losing their boy.'

Victoria stood back and surveyed the table and then counted out the number of goodies on the table. 'Three scones each, plus ham and stovies and christening cake, and I've enough gooseberries to go round. Pinch of sugar, a little milk off the top of the bottle – do you think there is any cream at the top of the milk these days, Nellie – and they'll be lovely.'

'Fit for a queen,' said Nellie proudly.

'It won't matter, Nellie,' said Victoria, 'wee Thomas James not having a father. Tell Flora to phone them.'

They said no more but instead began to wash all the cups and saucers and plates that would be needed for the party. These were all perfectly clean but still they would be washed and the sparkling silver would be cleaned. That was the way Catriona had always done things, and now Victoria and, she hoped, one day her own Mary Flora who would be coming to the party with her friend, Georges. Strange name, Georges, but say no more, Victoria, she warned herself.

The great day, the 14th of August, arrived and Victoria and Eddie stood on the lawn under the shade of their walnut tree and watched the cars of all their friends and neighbours, bustle up the driveway.

'Nice to have a party, Victoria,' said Eddie and took her hand.

Victoria clung to him for a second. 'You hate parties, you old fraud, but thanks. Here's mother. Help her with the cake, dear. Nancy. Help Granny with the cake, sweetheart.'

No time to think. Nellie, Tam, Flora and little Thomas James, as good as he had been that morning, walked up from the cottage and then car after car pulled into the steading and friends alighted and presented their offerings to Victoria and to the young mother. The last to arrive were the Inchmarnocks and Connie and Victoria knew, as soon as she saw them, that there was more than happiness at a baby's christening to account for their glowing looks.

'I have to tell Catriona, first Catriona,' whispered Lady Inchmarnock as she hugged Victoria. 'Sandy, you tell.'

But there was no need. His face told the story.

'Jamie?' said Victoria. 'He's alive. Oh thank God.'

'And Xandro,' said his lordship. 'Too long a story, Victoria, after the others leave we'll go into detail, but they're both alive. Xandro's in need of medical attention, not serious, but wouldn't you know that lad of mine, "Oh we won't be a bother, sir," says he to the officer who picked them up. "My mother runs Inchmarnock House. She'll be glad to take Flying Officer Cameron off your hands." They're on their way, on a train from Southampton.'

Flying Officer Cameron. My brother, thought Victoria. My brother is safe and we'll give him a home if he wants one.

'Come and see the horses,' said Nancy pulling at Lord Inchmarnock's sleeve.

'All right, Nancy, but I'm Thomas James's godfather and can't be too long.'

Victoria stood and watched them walk towards the paddock listening to Nancy, who had never addressed a word to Lord

326

Inchmarnock before her accident, chattering away about the horses and the baby and the christening cake.

'Where is Mary Flora and this Georges?' she asked herself angrily as she turned towards the house.

'It's that telephone again, Victoria,' called Nellie, splendid in *Jimmy's graduation dress,* 'and this time there's a voice.'

'It's them,' thought Victoria, her heart sinking. 'She's not coming home.'

With a heavy heart she walked into the house that was echoing with laughter and chatter and the crying of a baby, beautiful sounds, all of them. She picked up the receiver.

'Hello, Mary Flora.'

'Victoria, this is you, Victoria?'

She sat down as her knees gave way beneath her.

'Yes,' she managed. 'Yes, it's me.'

'This is Emil. You remember, please, you remember? I have not time. I wait for a plane but I ask you to help?'

'Help? Yes, of course, what can I do?'

'It is with much complication but my daughter, my Anneliese, she is free, Victoria, and she is arriving in Dundee tomorrow, with a Czechoslovakian boy and a German farmer. They are there but I am still here.'

The line went dead and she called into the receiver, 'Emil, Emil, can you hear me?'

There was no reply and she put the receiver back and immediately it rang again.

'The lines are bad,' his voice said. 'Victoria. They think I am there and I am still here. No-one else knows about Anne-liese. Please, you will go and bring them to your home. Tomorrow, the East Station, I think, in the morning, 7.30, and I will come soon. Tell my Anne...'

And this time the telephone went dead and it did not ring again.

'Bad news, Victoria?' It was Eddie.

'No, not bad. Good, but strange, I don't really understand.'

They stayed quietly in the kitchen while she told him about the telephone call.

'His daughter was in a concentration camp? And she's coming with a German?'

She could only nod.

'We'll fetch them, Victoria,' said Eddie easily. 'Plenty of room here till her father gets here. Wonderful story. Nice that something good has come out of this damned mess.'

'Look who we found walking up from the road,' said Lord Inchmarnock as he, Nancy and two other young people entered the kitchen.

Victoria held out her arms and her older daughter walked into them.

'Sweetheart,' said Victoria, 'I was so worried that you wouldn't get here.'

'You would not believe how difficult getting home has been,' said Mary Flora as she hugged her father and then at last there was time to look at the young man who stood awkwardly behind her.

'This is Georges,' said Mary Flora and her voice told her parents everything she felt about the slender young man. 'We want to get married but Georges is so European and insisted on talking to my papa first.' She pulled Georges forward. 'Here's my dad, Georges. Give him a cup of tea, Daddy, while I go in and say hello to everyone.'

She stopped at the door and looked back at her father seriously. 'Japan has capitulated, Daddy. The war is over. Isn't that wonderful.'

Eddie and Victoria looked at one another. Victoria knew that they were thinking the same things. The war was over. Jamie and Xandro were alive. Tomorrow they would offer a home even for a short time to European refugees and this old house would expand to shelter them all. Their daughter was to marry a foreigner, but what did that matter.

'I know what your grampa would have called today, Victoria,' smiled Eddie.

Victoria could hardly speak so happy was she. She nodded as she forced back her tears. 'A walnut shell day, Eddie, a real walnut shell day.'

The publishers hope that this book has given you enjoyable reading. Large Print Books are especially designed to be as easy to see and hold as possible. If you wish a complete list of our books please ask at your local library or write directly to:

Magna Large Print Books
Magna House, Long Preston,
Skipton, North Yorkshire.
BD23 4ND

This Large Print Book, for people
who cannot read normal print,
is published under the auspices of

THE ULVERSCROFT FOUNDATION

Other MAGNA Titles
In Large Print

LYN ANDREWS
Angels Of Mercy

HELEN CANNAM
Spy For Cromwell

EMMA DARCY
The Velvet Tiger

SUE DYSON
Fairfield Rose

J. M. GREGSON
To Kill A Wife

MEG HUTCHINSON
A Promise Given

TIM WILSON
A Singing Grave

RICHARD WOODMAN
The Cruise Of The Commissioner